Guilt Trip

Guilt Trip

The Weight of Being Ladoo

RAJANI TEWARI

NU VOICE
PRESS

NU VOICE PRESS

First published by NU VOICE PRESS 2025

An imprint of Hubhawks Pvt. Ltd
www.nuvoicepress.com

This is a work of fiction and all characters and incidents described in this book are the product of the author's imagination. Any resemblance to actual persons, living or dead, is entirely coincidental.

ISBN: 978-81-988726-1-6

Printed at Manipal Technologies Limited, Manipal

Published by: Nu Voice Press

To my ***son, Shlok****. May you always walk in your truth, fearless and unbowed, knowing that the world cannot define your worth.*

To my ***children, Shaurya and Shanaya****. You are my living prayers, my brightest hopes, my daily reminder that love is the greatest legacy.*

To my ***family****, thank you for the faith that held me up, for the love that never asked me to be anything but myself.*

To my ***brother****, your quiet strength has been a shelter in every storm.*

And to my ***divine guide, Lord Shiva****. In your infinite grace, I have found courage, surrender, and the peace that surpasses all understanding.*

PROLOGUE: GUILT – THE INVISIBLE LUGGAGE YOU NEVER DECLARED

Or how we all became unpaid carriers of emotional excess baggage

Pre-Boarding Notice

Before you fly into your life,
There's baggage packed by guilt and strife.
Not yours alone, it travels free,
In comments masked as sympathy.
Declare it now or keep it tight —
It weighs you down, though, out of sight.

We All Have That One Guilt. Or Nine.

MAYBE YOURS ARRIVED when you first saw your reflection and wondered if your arms were allowed to exist in sleeveless clothes.

Maybe it came when you dared to enjoy your work more than playdates.

Or maybe it bloomed in silence, in a room you never entered again after the test showed two lines... then none.

Guilt isn't linear. It's like a playlist on shuffle. Some days it sings, some days it screams.

But make no mistake, it's always there. Especially if you're a woman in India with opinions and ovaries.

Welcome to Flight 9G: Nine Guilts to Selfhood

Here's what this book is not:

- A self-help manual
- A motivational poster on mothering
- A polite memoir with sponsored subtlety.

This is a real trip. A *guilt trip.*

And like all memorable trips, there will be:

- Unexpected breakdowns
- Strange co-passengers

- ℵ Unwashed hair and overdrafted credit (of emotions, of course).

My Co-Pilot: Miss Guilt Herself

She has many faces:

- ℵ The aunty at the wedding buffet who says, "*Beta*, you still have time to lose weight."
- ℵ The Instagram mom who bakes vegan *ragi* cookies with flaxseed frosting
- ℵ The manager who thinks maternity leave is a paid vacation.

But most importantly? She sounds just like me.
"Am I doing enough?"
"Should I have kept quiet?"
"Was that selfish?"

Why This Book, Why Now

Because I was tired of being sorry. Tired of laughing off insults. Tired of making peace treaties with mirrors, baby bags, and Excel spreadsheets.

This isn't just my story. It's *our* story.

Every chapter holds a version of you:

- ℵ The version that overachieved just to be seen
- ℵ The version that wore smiles to cover scars

ℵ The version that danced at family functions while dying inside.

Silent Singh and the Airport Analogy

When I first spoke of this book, my partner, Silent Singh, said, "This is like airport security for the soul. You're finally checking what you packed by accident."

That's it. This isn't just my baggage check. It's yours too.

Let's open the damn suitcase together.

Writer's Note

This chapter is the pre-boarding gate of who we were before guilt arrived.

It gets messier. Funnier. Sadder. Truer.

And somewhere in between, you might just meet yourself again.

Because if life is a journey, then guilt is the excess baggage no one warned you about.

Now boarding. Seat belts are optional. The truth is mandatory.

Let's take off.

CHAPTER 1:

FLABBERGASTED BUT FABULOUS

Or how Ladoo Singh broke scales, stereotypes, and one plastic chair at a cousin's wedding.

"They tried to pinch her belly. She pinched reality instead."

Ode to the Girl Called Moti

They called her names, they weighed her pride,
They stared as if she couldn't hide.
But fat was not a flaw to mend,
She shaped her self-love to defend.
She wore her rolls like royal silk,
A toast to curves and honeyed milk.
Her name was Ladoo, sweet and round —
But oh, the strength in her rebound!

LADOO SINGH WAS never just "Ladoo." She was a walking mood board of metaphors people didn't ask for — *moti*, *golu*, a "pillow with legs", "healthy-looking," "voluptuous," and once, very kindly, "the sweet girl with... potential." Her name was used less often than adjectives about her body. She wasn't a person. She was a group chat subject, a Facebook comment thread, and once, a full-on WhatsApp family debate.

They had *opinions*. About her plate, her weight, her fate.

Aunties whispered like it was their cardio – "Such a *pretty face*, shame about the body."

(As if her thighs were personally offending God.)

Everyone pitched in like she was a crowd-funded identity:

- ℵ Her mom blamed hormones.
- ℵ Her dad blamed carbs.
- ℵ Her cousins blamed Netflix.
- ℵ Her uncle, who had no neck, suggested yoga.

Even the Uber driver chimed in: "Have you tried drinking hot water with lemon?"

Sir, focus on the road.

But while they fussed about her *figure*, they completely missed the *art*.

She was a piece from the Renaissance in a world obsessed with stick figures. A Rubens muse, reincarnated in sneakers and sarcasm.

Her face? Let's talk about that divine canvas.

Brows: arched like they were sculpted by Michelangelo's mood swings.
Lashes: so long they deserved their own postcode.

And her smile?

Please. That smile could turn therapy bills into punchlines. Soft dimples sat on either side like they were guarding a secret. Probably were.

She didn't just walk — she *waltzed.*

Her hips had rhythm, her thighs wrote poetry when she climbed stairs.
And her arms? Not "flabby," thank you very much.

They were *soft weapons*, built to cradle sobbing friends, overwatered plants, and the occasional existential crisis.

Her hair? – an ecosystem.

A textured, twisted, coiled masterpiece.

Each strand had a backstory. Each bun, a biography. She didn't straighten it; she *dared* it to do what it wanted.

Some days it was a forest, other days a revolution. Either way, it always arrived before she did.

She dressed like colour therapy met chaos theory and made it fashion.
Crop tops? Yes.

Bright patterns? Every damn day.

That one dress that made people pause and rethink their sexuality? Oh, it had a name. ("The Weapon.")

But the world kept trying to rename her.

"Fat."

Not as an adjective, but as a destiny.

As if "fat" was the full sentence, instead of a syllable in her novel.

They'd ask passive-aggressively, "Don't you want to be *healthy*?" (Translation: Don't you want to be *small enough to ignore?*) She'd smile, take a deep breath, and say, "My blood pressure's fine, Susan. But your jealousy is peaking."

What they didn't know:

She danced in her mirror to Beyoncé and *Bhajans.*

She made memes that ended friendships and built new ones.

She once stood up to a mansplainer so well, the patriarchy shook for three business days.

She was soft *and* sharp.

She could bake you banana bread and roast you in the same breath.

Her heart? Ridiculous.

She remembered your cat's birthday.

She sent "just checking in" texts like it was a spiritual practice. She carried stories — hers, yours, everyone's — and still had room to hold her own joy.

And yes, she was fat.

So what?

She was also fabulous.

Fearless.

Funny as hell.

She wasn't trying to be anyone's before-and-after.

She was the *during*. The *meanwhile*. The *magic*.

She wasn't just a person.

She was an event.

An entire *experience*.

And the world?

Still playing catch-up.

Weddings were her war zones. Sarees stitched with mirror work, aunties sharpened with microaggressions, and the buffet line moving faster than her self-esteem. Her earliest memories are of being the reluctant star in the family's fat joke circus. She'd enter a wedding hall and uncles would trumpet like elephants; not because they loved wildlife, but because *she* was the wildlife. Somewhere between the *gajar ka halwa* and glares from her *maasi*, Ladoo learned to shrink while taking up space.

Ladoo's cousins were ethereal, floating around like Bollywood breezes in *lehengas* that refused to crease. Meanwhile, she was sweating in silk, trying not to look like a maroon parachute.

And yet she smiled. Not because she was confident, but because sarcasm hadn't yet found its way to her baby teeth.

If there was a gathering of relatives, you could bet Ladoo would be cornered by someone offering unsolicited advice, always served with a *samosa.*

"*Beta*, still no *rishta*?"

"Such a pretty face! Imagine if you lost just a bit…" "Time is running out, no? You're not getting younger."

She once told an aunty, "Aunty, time isn't running out. It's I who's running late. For dessert."

That didn't go down well. The *gulab jamuns* did.

The Childhood of a Chubby Comet

Ladoo had always been "the big one." In school photos, she was always at the back. Not because she was tall, but because she blocked the view. Her teachers adored her. She was witty, bright, and quick to help. But her classmates saw her as a punchline with extra snacks. They mooed when she entered, laughed when she ran, and one boy even called her "Chubby Chewbacca." He got a tight slap — not from the teacher, but from Ladoo.

Revenge was served cold, like her leftover *aloo tikki.*

Her defence? Humour so sharp it could cut cholesterol. When someone asked, "Do you know how heavy you are?", she replied, "Yes, emotionally too."

You don't owe thinness to the world.

You don't owe silence to the mockery.

You owe yourself peace. And maybe *pani puri* on Tuesdays.

Family Portraits and Forgettable Frames

In every family photo, Ladoo was either cropped out or cropped behind. Her cousins glided through life like shampoo commercials, with their flowy hair, bouncy *lehengas*, and the metabolism of mountain goats. Ladoo? She prayed her blouse hook wouldn't fly off during the family dance.

During wedding seasons, she wasn't just judged — she was *evaluated.* One aunty literally patted her waist and said, "Hmm, little tight, *beta. Arey*, these young girls don't care now." To which Ladoo smiled and said, "Aunty, it's tight because I have boundaries. You should try some."

She wasn't just a person; she was a community project everyone had a comment on — family, friends, teachers, milkmen, and occasionally, Uber drivers. Most didn't see *her*; they saw a shape they'd been taught to critique. To them, she was *the fat girl*, as if that alone explained her, as if the word "fat" carried the full weight of her story. And for a while, she believed them. She memorised the art of shrinking — sucked in her stomach in family photos, laughed before they could, and wore black like it could make her invisible. Every joke they cracked, she absorbed like a bruise. But bruises heal, and she realised silence hurt more than sarcasm ever could.

So she sharpened her tongue. If the world was going to throw words like darts, she'd learn to catch them mid-air and fling them back, flaming. Her sass wasn't born cute. It was carved out of every awkward fitting room, every backhanded compliment, every moment someone said, "You've got such a pretty face," like the rest of her was a tragedy. Ladoo didn't wake up confident one morning. She built it from splinters — painful little pieces she stitched into armour. Now, when people try her, she answers not because she needs to win, but because she *can*. Because she decided a long time ago: if she's going to live in a world that won't stop staring, she might as well give them a damn show.

The Rishta Raids Begin

By her early twenties, Ladoo became *Shaadi Material*™. Her accomplishments, including gold medals, corporate career, and public speaking awards, were packaged under one reluctant line on matrimonial websites:

"Curvy but confident."

Translation: "Great girl, but please look past the paunch."

The latest blow came in the form of a "casual outing," which turned out to be a surprise appointment at a photo studio — her parents' latest ploy to get her listed on a matrimonial site. "Just a few nice pictures, *beta*," her mother said, clutching her *dupatta* like she was about to testify in court.

But at the studio, it became clear this wasn't about memories. It was marketing. The photographer, a man named Bunty who smelled like *chai* and compromise, took one look at Ladoo and asked if she wanted her "face shape adjusted."

Her father chimed in, "Just soften the jawline and make her cheeks a little less full." As if her cheeks were guilty of something. The full-length shots were even worse — waist cinched in, arms slimmed down, a little "brightening" to her skin tone, because apparently being fat and dark was two strikes too many.

Self-Deprecation: Ladoo's Safety Net

Ladoo became the funny one. Not the hot one, the mysterious one, the desirable one. Just the 'LOL Ladoo' who made boys laugh but never looked back.

The girl you called before exams, not before Valentine's.

She played the supporting role in her own story.

The Lie That Liked Her Back

One evening, Ladoo posted a photo online. Full filter. Slimming angle. Captioned: *"Feeling fit. Living light."*

The likes rolled in.

So did the guilt.

Because she wasn't fit, she wasn't light. She wasn't even sure if her jeans button was hanging by a thread. But the validation felt good. *Addictively* good. Until it felt fake.

That night, she looked in the mirror — not hunting for flaws, but gathering facts.

She saw a girl with layers; yes, on her body, but deeper still, in her soul: soft edges hiding sharp wit, warmth stitched with wildness, humour laced with history.

She leaned in close, eye to eye with her reflection, and whispered:

"I'm Ladoo Singh. I am soft. I am round. I am full of fire. And if I ever shrink, it'll be from laughter, not shame."

The Guilt Inventory

- The guilt of asking for a second helping.
- The guilt of laughing too loud.
- The guilt of wearing a sleeveless *kurta* when her arms felt like *parathas*.
- The guilt of being seen.

Each time she showed up, a voice inside whispered: *Too much. Too big. Too loud.*

But another voice, softer but stronger, whispered back: *Show up anyway.*

So she did.

She topped her exams, won inter-college debates, aced interviews, and bagged a great job without knowing Excel, but with excellent expressions. Still, every achievement was footnoted with a "but."

"She's doing well, but still unmarried."

"She's smart, but imagine if she lost weight."

"She's confident, but confidence isn't cuteness."

At work, her colleague, whom she usually always got along with and gossiped with, turned to her with a smile, and then added, "You know, you'd be perfect if you did keto."

Ladoo smiled and said, "You'd be perfect if you didn't speak."

When Laughter Was Armour

Act 1: The Early Grit — School Daze

Ladoo's room looked like a museum of overachievement:

- ℵ Trophies lined up like politicians during elections.
- ℵ Certificates filed by month, mood, and subject.
- ℵ Medals jingling from drawer handles like guilt-laced wind chimes.

To outsiders, she was thriving. To her? She was bargaining with self-worth.

"If I top the class, maybe they'll forget I'm fat."

"If I win first prize, maybe I'll be someone they invite to birthday parties."

Ladoo wasn't chasing excellence. She was trying to outrun rejection.

Her comedy was a shield, her sass a sword.

Behind every zinger was a girl who just wanted to be loved, without a disclaimer.

She remembered how even in her friend circle, she became the "funny one." Never the crush. Never the one being texted after the party. Just the one cracking jokes between two people flirting. She was the life of the party, and sometimes, its loneliest.

It started with **the dress**.

A deep maroon bodycon number with gold thread embroidery hugging all the right places. The kind of dress designed to whisper *I know I'm a vision,* not shout it. Ladoo bought it on a whim and against all generational advice. "Something looser would be more flattering," her mother had said, clutching a *dupatta* like it was a moral compass. Ladoo had smiled sweetly and bought the tightest thing in the store.

Because this time, she wasn't dressing to disappear. She was dressing to **declare**.

The night of the party, she did her liner sharp, her curls wild, her heels unapologetically loud. When she walked into the room, the music didn't stop, but heads did turn. Her friends shrieked and clapped, the way girls do when joy meets awe. Even the lighting seemed to cooperate.

She felt good. *Really* good. Not in a pretend-for-Instagram way. In a deep, grounded, *I-don't-owe-anyone-a-damn-thing* way.

Then he walked over.

Tall. Clean jawline. That kind of expensive-smelling cologne that whispered, *"My mother still does my laundry, but I can hold a conversation."*

"Hey," he said, with a smile like he had practised in mirrors. "You've got a great vibe going on."

Ladoo arched a brow. "Only *vibe*? Wow, and here I was hoping to give full fireworks."

He laughed, leaning in a little. "Actually… do you think you could introduce me to your friend? The one in the silver dress?"

There it was.

The thud.

The moment her insides went from sparkling champagne to flat soda.

For a flicker of a second, she felt twelve again. A girl in the schoolyard being asked to move aside so the popular boy could pass a note. Not to her, of course, but to the prettier girl beside her. History didn't always repeat, but it sure knew how to rhyme.

But this time, she didn't shrink.

She smiled. That sharp, polite kind of smile women develop after years of being the warm-up act for someone else's main show.

"Oh, *her*?" Ladoo asked, cool as crushed mint. "She left. Said something about not wasting perfume on misplaced attention."

He blinked. She winked. And walked away, her heels clicking like karma on linoleum.

At the bar, she ordered with flair. "Something red, bold, and undiluted. Like my mood."

The bartender nodded, probably used to dramatic women and their poetic thirst.

A gentle voice piped up from the corner stool. "Loved that line. You write, or are you just naturally dangerous?"

Ladoo turned to find an older woman in a sequined shawl and sneakers, sipping soda with a lemon slice and the confidence of someone who'd survived multiple fashion eras *and* their exes.

"I used to disappear into walls," the woman said. "Now I prefer walls that glitter."

Ladoo laughed, really laughed. The kind that comes from knowing someone sees you, not your outfit, not your friend, not your potential —*you*.

"I used to wait for someone to look at me like I mattered," Ladoo replied. "Now I just wait for the DJ to play my song."

The woman raised her glass. "To dancing with your damn self."

And so, Ladoo danced.

Not for the gaze, not for the gram, not even for the girls, but for the girl she used to be.

Because healing sometimes comes in heels.

And sometimes the most powerful moment at a party isn't being noticed. It's walking away when you're not.

The Turning Point

It wasn't a moment of rage or revolution.

It was a moment of stillness.

She was trying on clothes at a mall, struggling with zippers, sweating from effort and embarrassment. A little girl nearby stared and whispered to her mom, "She's fat." The mom hushed her, embarrassed. But Ladoo didn't flinch.

She had heard it all before — in schoolyards, on *rishta* sofas, even from tailor shops that dared to charge her extra for "double cloth."

But this time was different. She didn't have to take the hit in silence.

She walked over, knelt down, and looked the girl square in the eye. "Yes, I am. And I'm also brave. And funny. And tired of hiding."

The girl blinked. Not out of fear, but curiosity. Because here was a woman who didn't deny the word "fat." She owned it. Turned it into glitter.

The little girl smiled — the kind of smile that said: *I've never seen someone fat be so… shiny.*

And then she walked away, a little seed of unlearning quietly planted.

Because the truth is, girls are taught very early what "pretty" looks like. It's not in the textbooks — it's in the way aunties pinch cheeks only if they're slim, in the way mothers sigh at shopping mall mirrors, in the way Disney draws waistlines thinner than their plotlines.

From the time we take our first steps, we're handed a mirror shaped by capitalism, coloured by patriarchy, and sharpened with shame. It tells us we're wrong before we've even had the chance to ask who we are.

That little girl's whisper wasn't just a comment. It was a curriculum. One that Ladoo refused to be a part of.

And that refusal?

That was the revolution wrapped in a maroon bodycon dress.

Writer's Perspective

I've met Ladoo in mirrors, in waiting rooms, in college corridors.

She's the girl everyone jokes about, and no one really listens to.

Here's a truth few talk about: body shaming doesn't just bruise the ego. It relocates your personality into survival mode. You start pre-empting jokes, dimming your glow, becoming the comedian before they make you the punchline.

I became the class clown — not because I loved attention, but because deflection was my cardio.

The mirror became a minefield. Clothes became negotiations. Compliments felt suspicious. Every "You're brave" sounded like "You're fat but functional."

But here's what I've learned:

The heaviest thing a woman can carry is guilt.

And Ladoo carried it with grace and glitter.

Inner Voice Note

"You are not your size. You are your story. And yours is worth more than inches and filters."

Chapter 2:

Gold Medals & Emotional Scars

Or how Ladoo Singh earned straight A's and crooked guilt lines.

"She was told to be everything. So she forgot to be herself."

Guilt Diploma

She earned degrees, not just in class,
But in shrinking dreams to let time pass.
She topped the test, yet lost her name,
To praise wrapped tight in guilt and shame.
But in her pause, she saw it true —
She wasn't broken, just overdue.
To fail in peace, to laugh unplanned,
To write her worth in her own hand.

LADOO SINGH'S REPORT cards were always laminated before they even left the school gate. Not by her, but by her parents, who'd parade them at weddings, funerals, and anywhere with more than five adults in attendance.
She wasn't just smart. She was *topper smart.*
The kind that got 99 and still felt like a failure because someone else got 99.2.

The kind who aced quizzes but flunked self-love.

Because beneath every "Well done!" was a whispered "Now what?"

The Childhood Gold Rush

At age 10, Ladoo had already won three essay competitions, two dance contests (where she didn't even move much, just expressive eyes), and a spelling bee where she corrected the judge.

Her father beamed. "My daughter is a genius."

Her mother? "Genius is good. But girls shouldn't be too loud about it."

By 13, she had absorbed two opposing truths:

- Be the best.
- Don't make others uncomfortable about it.

She learned to shine softly.
Like a disco ball dimmed for guests.

Ladoo's Diary, Tuesday, 8:03 AM

Breakfast: 3 half-burnt *parathas.*
Makeup: Concealer of guilt.
Bag: Laptop, lunchbox, and one stuffed unicorn.
Mood: Somewhere between "I've got this" and "I've lost it."
Welcome to the Ladoo Express. Next stop: Sharma Ma'am's judgment, followed by Excel Hell, and a bonus guilt trip through Forgot-the-PTM Land.

Achievement: The Trap Dressed as a Trophy

She entered adolescence with certificates and medals, but they didn't decorate her soul. They weighed it down.

She smiled through exhaustion. Cried over a 94%.

Her friends envied her.

Her teachers adored her.

Her classmates? "Teacher's pet."

Relatives? "Your daughter is our benchmark."

And Ladoo? She was quietly suffocating under the weight of her own potential.

She once got a B in Chemistry.

Her mother's silence that evening was louder than any scolding. Even the *papad* cracked nervously.

Flashback: The First Crack

Ladoo was 11. School Annual Day. She was cast in a "Butterfly Ballet." Everyone got flowy wings.

She was cast as... the tree. "Because you're strong and solid," the teacher said. But even at 11, Ladoo knew tree was code for *not thin enough to fly*.

Her leaves kept falling. So did her self-worth.

Act 2: College: Hustle, Hype, and Heartburn

College felt like adulthood with unpaid internships and vending machine therapy.

Ladoo joined every club. She led every project. She wrote winning essays with fingers that trembled from caffeine.

One night, she got a perfect GPA and burst into tears; not from joy, but from sheer *exhaustion*.

Body by Society™

Ladoo wasn't just body-shamed. She was body-branded.

- Relatives made her the punchline.
- Classmates made her invisible.
- Brands made her feel like beauty was a reward for shrinking.

So she became the clown who cracked jokes before anyone else could. If you laughed *with* her, maybe you wouldn't laugh *at* her.

Degree 1: Guilt of Being Better

The better she did, the lonelier she felt.
She watched as cousins whispered behind her back:
"She thinks she's too smart."
"Who's she trying to impress?"
"She'll struggle to find a match."
Smartness in boys was sexy.
In girls? Suspicious.
One uncle said, "She's so brainy, but a bit aggressive, *na*?" Ladoo replied, "Aggression is my cardio, *chachu*."

Degree 2: Guilt of Being Busy

At 22, she landed a plush job.
Celebrations lasted 3 hours before the questions began:
"Will she shift cities?"
"Will she miss her cousin's engagement?"
"Will she still cook every Sunday?"
At a family function, her absence was noted as a crime.
"She's too career-oriented," someone muttered.
Ladoo wanted to yell, "I missed a wedding, not my values!"

But instead, she replied with a gift: an air fryer and an apology.

Degree 3: Guilt of Earning More

When her first salary came, Ladoo took her parents out for dinner.

The waiter gave her the bill.

Her father chuckled, "Our daughter's paying now!"

But at home, when she suggested a new fridge, her aunt whispered, "So ambitious. Girls shouldn't earn *more* than their husbands. It upsets the balance."

Balance. As if ambition were an earthquake and she was the Richter scale.

Degree 4: Guilt of Saying No

She once said no to a *puja*.

It clashed with a client meeting.

Her cousin said, "All this modern lifestyle has ruined our values."

Ladoo looked up from her laptop and said, "My bank balance disagrees."

But inside, guilt simmered.

Because girls are taught to bend like yoga poses nobody asked for.

Corporate Darling, Closet Crumbler

Her boss once said,
"You're a machine, Ladoo."
She smiled.
And cried in the washroom, silently.
Because she wasn't a machine.
She was a woman on four hours of sleep, one banana, and a will stronger than WiFi.
She once asked for a mental health day.
Manager: "Is it urgent?"
Ladoo: "Yes. My sanity is slipping into Outbox."

While society measured me in kilos, my workplace measured me in KPIs. Thankfully.

In the office, I was known as the "pitch queen" because I could sell sand in a desert and sarcasm in a shareholders' meeting. My PowerPoints had more personality than most people's dating apps.

One manager told me, "You don't let your weight affect your work."

I replied, "You don't let your face affect your confidence either. Inspiring."

HR scheduled a feedback session for the next day.

Joy ≠ Guilt-Free

One weekend, she treated herself to a spa day.
Posted a story: *"Me time = best time."*

That evening, a cousin sent a meme: *"When you relax while your mom still does all the work."*

Ladoo laughed.
Then blocked her.

The Laundry Breakdown

It wasn't a big moment.
No drama. No tears.
She was folding clothes on a Sunday evening.
Looking at three piles — office, home, gym (lol).
And suddenly whispered:
"How did I become a checklist instead of a person?"
That night, she didn't make to-do lists.
She made a "don't-do" list:

- ℵ Don't apologise for resting.
- ℵ Don't say yes to *pujas* you don't enjoy.
- ℵ Don't downplay your win to soothe someone else's ego.

The Pause Revolution

She bought flowers.
No occasion.
She took herself out to dinner.
No company.
She ordered dessert first.
And laughed so loud, even her guilt paused for breath.

Writer's Perspective

Ladoo Singh didn't collect degrees — she collected doubts.

Not because she lacked confidence, but because everyone around her packaged guilt with praise.

She wasn't overachieving. She was overcompensating.

For approval. For belonging. For not rocking the boat.

This chapter is a gentle roar: You don't owe the world a version of you they're comfortable with.

Inner Voice Note

"You don't owe perfection to anyone. Not your family, not your job, not your partner. You owe yourself joy."

Chapter 3:

Rishta Roulette: Chai, Lies & Aunties' Eyes

Or how Ladoo Singh survived the arranged marriage circus without murdering anyone with a samosa.

"She wasn't looking for a husband. She was looking for someone who wouldn't ask her to become less."

Rishta Rebellion

Bring the tray, adjust the smile,
Walk like grace, hide the guile.
Offer tea, not your truth,
Lie a little, seem uncouth.
Ask no questions, blink not twice,
Shrink your dreams to fit their price.
But then she rose, no veil, no fear,
And said: "The right one will see me clear."

IF WILD SAFARIS involved polyester *sarees*, gold bangles clanking like alarm bells, and judgmental looks sharper than trimmers at a beauty salon, then welcome to the Indian arranged marriage setup — a thrilling wildlife experience where Ladoo Singh was always the main attraction.

By the time I hit 24, I had a PhD in Rejection and an MBA in Matrimonial Humiliation. *Rishta* aunties would come armed with questions, comments, and passive-aggressive compliments.

"Pretty face, just need to tone down a little."

Tone down? Lady, this isn't a soprano solo.

One hopeful bachelor's mother asked, "Can she cook and lose weight?"

I smiled sweetly and said, "Only one dish — self-respect stew. Want a taste?"

Needless to say, the alliance evaporated faster than my will to attend another biodata parade.

At 26, Ladoo had become what society lovingly called *Shaadi Material.* But like cheap nylon, that material was expected to stretch around egos, absurd expectations, and waistlines shrinking faster than self-worth. She has officially entered into the "Marriageable Age" Hunger Games, where the stakes were high, the snacks were stale, and the prize was… adjusting forever.

Rishta rounds came like episodes of a reality show no one asked to be on: *The Bachelorette: Indian Edition (Arranged, Filtered, and Fully Funded by Relatives).*

Ladoo started keeping score.

Round One: The Pilot Episode

The boy's family walks in, bearing sweets and scrutiny.
Aunty-in-chief opens with the classic: "Pretty face, just need to tone down a little."
Tone down? Lady, this isn't a soprano solo.
Score: 4/10. Lost major points for body-shaming with a smile.

Round Two: The Compatibility Quiz

The boy liked hiking. I liked not sweating.
He wanted "a low-maintenance girl."
I asked, "You mean emotionally or financially?"
He blinked like I'd spoken Sanskrit.
Score: 3/10. Decent jawline, but unfortunately allergic to nuance.

Round Four: The One with Too Many Allergies

No onions, no garlic, no feminism.
He looked at me like I was an overripe mango — possibly sweet, but best used in *chutney*.
Score: 0/10. Unsubscribe.

Bonus Round: The Ghosting Guru

Met him once. Thought we vibed.
He disappeared. His mother texted *my* mother to say I had "too much personality."
Sorry, should I have left it in the fridge?

Each visit blurred into the next. The same questions, same checklist, same thinly veiled horror when they realised Ladoo had opinions *and* curves. Apparently, wanting respect *and rasmalai* was too ambitious.

Eventually, she stopped dressing up for them. She wore what she wanted, said what she meant, and smiled only when she felt like it. And if they didn't want the full-fat, full-volume, fire-in-her-eyes version of her?

Well then, their loss.

This isn't a clearance sale.

It's a limited edition.

The Lie That Broke Me

At 27, tired of being ignored, I told someone on a *rishta* call that I worked with a foreign firm in London.

He replied, "Impressive. We like girls who've gone abroad. They return more... refined."

Refined?! Like basmati rice?

I laughed on the call. And cried for two days after.

I wasn't ashamed of my truth. I was ashamed that it wasn't *marketable.*

Welcome to the Great Indian *Rishta* Circus.

Where my biodata was served like samosas — crisp on top, soft inside, with a filling of crushed self-esteem.

I was the girl they *almost* picked.

- "She's smart, but *thodi* healthy hai."
- "Nice girl. But can she cook nine types of *paratha*?"
- "*Beta*, have you tried yoga? It's good for your... frame."

Mirror, mirror on the wall, who's the most dieted of them all?

Every week, I put on a new *kurta*, pasted on a polite smile, and became the heroine of a low-budget *shaadi* pilot that never got renewed. My mother would whisper, "Just smile and don't argue."

I'd nod while sipping *chai* and silently critique their furniture, taste in curtains, and the fact that the groom thought 'feminist' was a type of pasta.

Ladki Dekhne Ka Season

There are wedding seasons, mango seasons, and then there's the "*rishta dekhne ka*" season. This peculiar Indian mating dance begins with a phone call from a distant aunty who hasn't spoken to your family since your *mundan* ceremony but now claims spiritual responsibility for your future.

She calls my mom: "*Sarla, suna Ladoo MBA kar rahi hai? Arey wah. Mera bhanja bhi US se aaya hai. Dono ki jodi bilkul Lajpat Nagar aur branded suit jaisi lagegi.*" ("Did you hear? She's doing her MBA now. And my nephew's just back from the US. Those two would look like high street fashion meets bridal bazaar.")

Decoded: Functional, flashy, and stitched to impress.

Cut to: Me, scrubbed pink with a facial, eyes lined with enough kajal to write the *Mahabharat*, wearing a *dupatta* that behaves like it has stage fright. I'm seated with teacups, tray, and tension.

The Great Indian Rishta Script

Here's what happens at every setup:

1. **Family enters.**

The girl is told to smile, not too much — just the right "*sanskari*" amount.

2. ***Chai* arrives.**

Bonus points if she doesn't spill while walking in heels on marble floors.

3. **Interrogation begins.**

Questions include:

- Can you cook? (Translation: Will you serve me forever?)
- Can you relocate? (Translation: Will you give up your career?)
- What are your hobbies? (Translation: How traditional are you?)

4. **Post-interrogation whispers.**

"She's nice, but…"
ALWAYS. THE. BUT.
"She's nice, but bigger than expected."
"She's nice, but talks a lot."
"She's nice, but too modern."
"She's nice, but can she smile less?"

The Bio-Data Betrayal

Ladoo's biodata was the stuff of dreams: MBA, corporate success, inter-college winner, witty as hell.

But the family description changed like a bad ad campaign.

Before: "Ambitious, well-travelled, working professional."
After six rejections: "Homely. Flexible. Ready to adjust."

She once saw her own photo printed with a caption: *"Loves family. Open to compromises. Very cooperative."*

She felt like a discounted sofa on OLX.

The Dietitian Proposal

The absolute winner was one family who showed up with a dietitian.

"We want to help her become the best version of herself," the boy's mother smiled, handing Ladoo a pamphlet for "Slim & Shine."

Ladoo flipped the pamphlet, nodded sincerely, and said, "Wonderful. Do you have one for outdated mindsets?"

Her parents were mortified.

But Ladoo? She was done.

Aunty Fatigue and the Scale of Self-Worth: Meet the Auntyverse™

Population: Loud. Opinionated. Perfumed with unsolicited advice.

Aunty #1: Smells like fairness cream and judgment.

Aunty #2: Specialises in toxic compliments. "Your face is so pretty... if only you lost a little weight."

Aunty #3: The Diet Drill Sergeant. Once handed me a papaya during a wedding buffet. *"Beta, dessert ke jagah yeh le lo. Yeh glowing deta hai."* ("Sweetheart, have this instead of dessert. It's supposed to bring out your glow.")

What broke her wasn't the rejections — it was her own mother's voice, one quiet evening, after another family said no.

"Maybe just lose a little, *beta.* They're not wrong."

That sentence hit like a betrayal dipped in affection.

Her whole life, she had fought the world with jokes and jabs, but when the fire came from home, it burned differently.

She didn't cry.

She didn't scream.

She ordered butter chicken and posted a gym selfie.

Caption:

*"Running out of f*cks to give. Full cardio."

Match Found (Almost)

Then came Boy 7.

Kind. Smart. Didn't blink at her size.

Said, "I love your energy and confidence."

She nearly sighed in relief.

Then came the sentence that snapped it.

"You know, if you lost 5-6 kilos, you'd be perfect."

PERFECT.

She put down her fork, wiped her mouth, and smiled:

"I already am."

Then walked out of that restaurant like it was a runway and she was the damn finale.

Writer's Perspective

This chapter isn't about boys.

It's about *buts.*

Every "but" is a ceiling women are told to duck under. And Ladoo didn't want to duck anymore.

She wanted to dance, with full arm fat jiggling if it had to.

She didn't want a partner who measured her worth in kilos. She wanted one who could handle the weight of her wit, her dreams, and her silence.

Inner Voice Note

"Don't shrink to fit into a frame they built. Build your own damn wall and hang your own portrait."

Chapter 4:

Silent Singh Speaks Louder

Where unsaid things scream the loudest, and love folds the laundry.

Love Without Sound Effects

He never said "forever" in glowing prose,
He just fixed the bulb when the hallway froze.
He never penned lines or rhymed my name,
But knew every flavour of my mood swing game.
No grand serenade, no dramatic sky —
Just quiet loyalty. And that's why I fly.

BY THE TIME Ladoo, aka I, had survived the matrimonial circus, I was about ready to throw in the towel on *all* men — Mr. Right, Mr. Wrong, Mr. Maybe-I'll-Call-You-Back, and Mr. Definitely-Not-My-Problem. I wasn't just jaded; I was practically a cynic with a PhD in disappointment. Love stories felt like fairy tales where everyone forgot to mention the part about endless rejection, unsolicited advice, and awkward biodata exchanges.

I had come to accept that *maybe* my soulmate was a myth invented by Bollywood screenwriters and desperate aunties. Maybe, just maybe, I was destined to be the star of my own solo show — one part sass, two parts stubbornness, and an infinite loop of "next, please."

Then, on a rainy Saturday afternoon, I found myself at a small art exhibit — the kind with abstract paintings that make you question your eyesight and a café that served questionable *chai* but great company.

That's where I saw him.

Silent Singh.

Not because he was mute — no, he was the opposite. Just emotionally WiFi-enabled and Bluetooth-averse. He spoke in gestures, glances, and carefully rationed syllables, like words cost him frequent flyer miles.

I, on the other hand, was all drama and delivery. A walking Broadway show with dialogue, soliloquies, and the occasional mic drop.

Where I was a burst of fireworks, Silent Singh was the punctuation. Usually a full stop. Sometimes a question mark.

We both stood, staring at the same painting — a swirl of colours that looked like a toddler's tantrum.

"You see chaos," I said, "I see a mess."

He shrugged, eyes meeting mine for a fraction longer than polite.

"Maybe that's life," he said, voice low and steady, "A beautiful mess."

In that moment, amidst spilt *chai* and half-baked interpretations of art, I realised I had no hope left for Mr. Right or Mr. Wrong. But maybe, just maybe, there was room for Silent Singh.

He doesn't say 'I love you'. He resets the router when I am about to have an emotional breakdown.

Reader, I married him before he could change the password.

The Man, The Mute, The Myth

He doesn't do roses. He fixes leaking taps at 1 AM because I can't sleep with drips.

He doesn't do romantic quotes. He downloads memes that remind him of my eye rolls.

He doesn't believe in fighting. He believes in pausing, breathing, and muting the TV.

Silent Singh has the emotional intelligence of a Himalayan monk trapped in the body of a man who can't find his socks unless they're screaming.

His Superpowers? Selective Hearing and Perfect Timing

Me: "I think I've gained weight again."

He looks up slowly, deadpan, "Gravity is working overtime for all of us."

Me: "Do you even listen when I talk?"

He blinks: "I've memorised your talking rhythm. I tune in around every 7th sentence. Worked so far."

Me: "Why don't you ever say sweet things like other husbands?" He grins: "Because I'm not like other husbands. I'm yours. That's a full-time job."

Reader, I didn't slap him. I made him *paratha*.

He didn't post #CoupleGoals selfies. He showed up when the world didn't. His humour was drier than a Gujarati *khakhra* but perfect for my moist, melodramatic soul.

When I asked, "Do I look fat in this?"

He said, "You look like Ladoo. That's who I fell for. Not Photoshop."

Reader, I married him.

Anger Issues? More Like Anger Tissues

His anger isn't volcanic. It's crockpot-level. Slow-simmering, stewing with silent resentment and clean-up anxiety.

He doesn't shout. He reorganises the fridge.

His version of yelling is passive-aggressively doing the dishes at 2 AM.

Me? I'm a word geyser. I erupt in metaphor and volume. He just raises one eyebrow, and it's the end of the argument. The eyebrow has spoken.

His Love Language: Action. Not Caption.

He never updates his relationship status.

He updates the WiFi when I'm on a deadline.

He forgets anniversaries but never forgets the brand of chips I eat when I'm low.

He doesn't say "I love you."

But once, during flu season, he watched 11 back-to-back episodes of my trashy drama series and didn't even mock it.

That's not just love. That's marital sainthood.

Why I Fell for His Silence

Because his silence is safe.

It's not cold — it's spacious.

In a world where people scream their opinions like broken loudspeakers, he's my library. Quiet, warm, and always open.

He lets me be the chaotic windchime I am — clanging, chiming, chimichanga-ing — while he holds the hook steady.

The Day I Truly Saw Him

It was one of those days. I had PMS, a presentation, a pimple, and people problems.

I came home and ranted for 42 minutes straight. He sat there, nodding occasionally, sipping *chai.*

Then, he left the room.

I thought, "Wow. Just walked off?"

He returned with *garam bhindi ki sabzi* (hot okra vegetable dish) a hot water bag, and the TV remote already tuned to my comfort movie.

That day, I realised:

Some people don't say "I'm here."

Inner Voice Note:

"He doesn't complete me. I was whole before. But he holds my pieces like they matter.

He doesn't 'fix' me. He tightens the bolts and leaves room for expansion.

Sometimes love doesn't shout. Sometimes, it just plugs in the charger quietly."

Writer's Sasspective

Silent Singh is not the hero they write about in books. He doesn't own a horse. He owns a toolkit.

He's not a man of words. He's a man of WiFi passwords, backup plans, and morning *chai*.

And when the world turns into a noisy, nosy, judgy fish market, he's the calm corner where I can sit, snack, and just be me.

Sometimes love doesn't echo.
It hums.

Chapter 5:

Thanks for Your Concern, I Miscarried and Made Chai

Because nothing says recovery like samosas and suffering in silence.

"She wore kajal, made tea, and carried a grief no one dared name — because silence is more socially acceptable than sadness."

"Spoiler Alert: I Lost the Plot"

Two pink lines, then Pinterest boards,
Dreams of onesies, baby chords.
Week nine came with a deafening hush,
And suddenly, joy turned to crushed.
Relatives came with laddoos and lore,
Told me I'm strong, while I scrubbed the floor.
Their words were sweet; their empathy was fried,
I smiled, served *chai*… and quietly died.

Ladoo's Diary: A Letter to Her Uterus

DEAR UTERUS,

You had one job.

I mean, seriously. I nourished you with *haldi doodh*, spinach, and hope. And this is what you do?

Still, no hard feelings.

Just a broken heart, a confused husband, and a fridge full of folic acid.

Scene: The Great Indian Miscarriage Management

"Don't cry too much, *beta* — it'll block your tubes."

"Maybe it was your job stress?"

"You should've done that *puja* with aunty."

Everyone had advice.

No one had space.

She wasn't allowed to mourn — just move on.

And while they debated astrology charts, she quietly deleted her baby name app.

Nobody prepares you for the silence. Not the hospital forms. Not the sympathetic smiles. Not even the doctor who avoids eye contact.

One second you're pregnant. The next, you're just... not.

The world doesn't pause for miscarriage. It hiccups in confusion. "Oh... that's so sad. At least you're young. Try again." *Try again.* Like it was a recipe that failed. A dish that didn't rise. A project that can be resubmitted.

But what about the grief that doesn't show? What about the guilt that leaks in between periods of numbness?

Vacuum in a Crowded Room

I walked through daily life like I was wrapped in bubble wrap. Protected. Distant. Pop-able.

People around me laughed. I smiled. Sort of. But nothing reached me.

Not the food. Not the music. Not even my favourite memes.

I was present. But I wasn't *there.*

Silent Singh, The Unmoving Pillar

He didn't cry. He didn't flinch. He didn't say sorry, or fix it, or philosophise.

He just *was.* Next to me. Behind me. With me.

On the night I lay staring at the ceiling, I whispered, "I think my body failed."

He replied,

"No. The world did. For making you believe it's your fault."

That was his thing. He let silence breathe. Not suffocate.

The Unsaid Pain

Everyone expected me to bounce back. ASAP. Like it was a cancelled vacation. Like my womb had a refresh button.

But I had named the baby. In my mind, she had eyes like mine.

Even though I had never met her, I missed her. And that is the kind of loss you can't share over *chai.*

Monologue: Ladoo vs. The Grief Gloss-over Committee

They said, "It's common."

Cool. So are mosquitoes. Doesn't mean I invite them in.

They said, "You can try again."

I said, "Try swapping your heart for a vacuum cleaner and let me know how that feels."

They said, "You need closure."

I said, "I need pizza, a pillow fort, and a break from patriarchy."

Scene: Cousin's Baby Shower

She attended. In a pretty *saree.*

Smiled. Complimented the crib. Laughed at baby name debates.

Inside?

She wanted to scream,

I had one too — a name, a dream, a cradle in my Amazon cart.

A tiny bassinet bookmarked between guilt and hope. A list full of rattles and rompers, of lullabies she'd never get to hum. She had already imagined the baby's laugh, its milky breath, the soft socks with giraffes on them.

She had, in a weak moment, even picked out the wallpaper — mustard moons and sleepy stars — for a nursery that now only existed as a ghost folder on her phone.

But instead, she passed the kachoris.

Because the guests had come, and the tray had to be full, and grief — well, grief was only allowed in bedrooms and bathroom stalls.

Not under fairy lights, not with people commenting on how glowing she looked in that *saree.*

No one talks about the miscarriage once the blood has dried. People ask, *"How's your health now?"* with that sideways pity, but they don't really wait for the answer.

They assume recovery is just about the body, not the soul. They assume a woman who's laughing at a party must've moved on.

But the truth is, she didn't move on.

She moved *with* it.

The emptiness walked beside her in every room, silent, respectful, well-dressed.

And yet, never once did it carry a tray.

So she did.

With grace. With lipstick. With shaking hands.

Because sometimes, love gets no closure.

It just gets quietly plated with *chutney* and served warm.

Her inner voice, soft as the space that once held her baby, murmured:

"They think I'm strong because I smiled."

"But strength is what held me when the cradle didn't."

And with that, she passed another plate.

Because sometimes, the bravest thing a woman can do is carry on, while carrying everything no one else can see.

Because women bleed quietly, and society likes its tragedy… well-behaved.

The Society of Shortcuts

"Don't think too much."

"Everything happens for a reason."

"Be positive."

No one says:

"It's okay to be angry. To be sad. To be selfish with your sorrow."

But Silent Singh did. He made soup. He switched off the news. He sat beside me while I cried over ads with laughing babies.

He even punched a wall once. Not dramatically. Just once. A controlled detonation.

"This wasn't fair," he said. That was his version of a breakdown.

When the Body Betrays the Soul

Every ache felt like punishment. Every cycle a cruel reminder.

I began writing letters I never sent: To the baby. To my uterus. To myself.

I kept one of them:

"Dear me, you did not fail. You carried love. You carry it still."

The Return

Healing isn't an event. It's the decision to wake up anyway. To laugh once. Then again. To eat a mango without crying. To forgive your own biology.

Silent Singh never said, "Move on." He said, "Move with it." And we did. With a dent. With a scar. But also with a story.

Grief is lonely. But pretending you're okay? That's like throwing a party for ghosts and realising you're the only one dancing.

So one evening, when my brain felt like a tangled headphone cord and my heart resembled a soggy *samosa*, I decided to reclaim my sanity in the most rebellious way possible: I bought a tiny jasmine plant. Because if life was going to hand me lemons, I was at least going to grow some flowers to sip tea beside.

Every morning, I watered that stubborn little green warrior and whispered sweet nothings to it — promises to be less of a hot mess and more of a slow-burning candle. Healing, I realised, isn't about giant leaps or perfect Pinterest moments; it's about tending to your own garden, even if half the time you're just hoping it doesn't die on you.

And just like that, between the awkward conversations with a plant and my ongoing battle with the universe, I started to feel a little less like a broken record and more like a remix — flawed, funny, and fiercely, unapologetically me.

Inner Voice Note:

"Grief is lonely. But pretending you're okay is lonelier."

Writer's Note

This chapter is not a tragedy. It's an elegy. To a moment. A maybe.

To the women who miscarried: You are still mothers. You are still whole.

Even when the cradle is empty. Even when the silence is loud. Even when the world forgets.

You remember. And that love? It never leaves.

Chapter 6:

Milk Stains & Meeting Invites

Or how Ladoo Singh breastfed, budgeted, and battled burnout — often at the same time.

"Her heels clicked through office corridors, her heart beat in the crib. And somehow, she still showed up for both."

Milk Stains & Metrics

The boardroom buzzed, her phone lit bright,
A baby's cry cut through the night.
She zipped her coat, then zipped her soul,
To juggle warmth and workplace role.
With files in hand and milk-stained chest,
She walked the world, still doing her best.
A mom in heels, a heart in sling —
She wore her guilt like angel wings.

LADOO SINGH HAD always been a multitasker. But no one warned her that one day, she'd be on a conference call discussing revenue targets while simultaneously rocking a baby, leaking milk, and Googling "why is my baby's poop green?"

Welcome to Motherhood: The Corporate Edition.

There was no orientation. No manual. No HR training on how to survive sleepless nights, swollen feet, cracked nipples, and spreadsheets.

She was now a mother.

She was now a working woman.

She was now walking guilt on two legs and a tired uterus.

From Boardroom to Breast Pump

Three months after delivery, Ladoo returned to work.

Not because she was ready. But because maternity leave had expired, like her favourite pair of pre-baby jeans.

Her body had changed. Her life had changed. But her job expectations? Same as ever.

She wore her favourite pantsuit on her first day back. It didn't fit. Her belly remembered what her boss had forgotten: she'd given birth. Not taken a vacation.

She stuffed tissues in her bra to soak up leaking milk and typed emails like a woman on a mission. Because she was.

The Morning Shift That Never Ends

Here was a typical morning:

- ℵ Baby cried at 3 AM.
- ℵ Baby refused the bottle at 4 AM.
- ℵ Baby decided sleep was for losers at 5:30 AM.
- ℵ Ladoo joined a Zoom meeting at 9:00 AM with one eye open, one boob out, and coffee that had been reheated twice.

And yet, she smiled.
Because smiling was cheaper than therapy.

The Return to Work: Sans Applause

Nobody clapped when she returned. There was no "Welcome Back, Warrior Mama" banner. Just back-to-back calls, tighter deadlines, and passive-aggressive colleagues whispering:
"She's not as fast as before."
"Motherhood changes priorities."
"She must be distracted."
She wanted to shout:
"Of course I'm distracted! I made a human, and now I have to make Excel sheets that make sense?"
But instead, she smiled.
And powered through.

Guilt, The Double-Sided Coin

If she stayed late at work, she felt guilty about missing bedtime.

If she left early, she felt guilty about leaving work hanging.

If she looked too happy, someone said, "Wow, you're really enjoying being away from the baby, huh?"

If she looked tired, someone said, "You should consider slowing down."

She couldn't win.

Motherhood had no medals.

Only mental load.

Monologue: Ladoo on Guilt

Working moms don't get holidays. We get tagged in memes.

And invited to mommy groups where everyone brings homemade millet laddoos, while I bring store-bought guilt in a Ziploc.

My phone has more parenting podcasts than playlists.

And my calendar has more guilt slots than growth goals.

But hey, I still showed up, didn't I?

Guilt Comes in Tiffins

The guilt isn't loud. It's sneaky.

It hides in school WhatsApp groups with messages like "Moms, please send a handwritten card today."

It whispers when you're clapping for someone else's child while your own waits at home.

It shouts when you get that text: "Mumma, where are you?"

A Scene from Ladoo's Life: PTM Day

Teacher: "Your child is bright, but he seems distracted."

Ladoo: "Yes, he gets it from me. I'm a high-functioning chaos coordinator."

Another mom says she baked cookies for the class.

Ladoo thinks of the packet of Hide & Seek in her bag and smiles; guilt tastes like chocolate today.

What They Don't Tell You

No one warns you that being a working mom means:

Knowing your colleagues better than your child's best friend.

Getting praised at work but ghosted by your own expectations.

Sitting in meetings planning year-end goals… and realising you missed your kid's first solo bike ride.

The Metrics of a Mom

She kept score in silence:

- ℵ Number of diapers changed: 11
- ℵ Number of PowerPoint slides finished: 18
- ℵ Number of times she cried in the washroom: 2
- ℵ Number of times she pretended to be okay: Infinity.

One day, her manager asked, "Can we schedule the meeting at 8 AM?"

She wanted to say, "Sure, if my baby agrees not to poop till 9." Instead, she said, "Absolutely."

And then silently screamed into a pillow.

When Moms Multitask Like Magicians

Ladoo once pitched a million-rupee campaign while her baby was latched on one side, and the maid was yelling in the background. She still closed the deal.

She once changed a diaper mid-presentation.

She once muted herself during a client call to sing "Twinkle Twinkle". Not for her baby, but for her own peace.

The Multitasking Lie

They say working mothers "do it all."

What they don't say is:

She's answering emails while her child yells "I have to PEE!" in aisle 5 of the supermarket.

Her Zoom background is blurred, not for professionalism, but to hide toy tornadoes.

She'll nail the boardroom pitch, but forget it's Fancy Dress Day. Her child goes as "Disappointment."

The Myth of "Balance"

They told her to "find balance."

So, she tried:

6:30 AM: Yoga

7:00 AM: Yelling

8:00 AM: Cooking

9:00 AM: Crying

10:00 AM: CEO Meeting

Balance?

More like circus tightrope walking in heels with a diaper bag in one hand and a KPI chart in the other.

Her In-laws: The Background Commentary: Guilt Served Hot, with *Ghee*

The pressure to be "nice" is sautéed into every *desi* woman's upbringing:

Never roll your eyes, just roll the *chapatis.*

Don't disagree. Just nod and burn quietly like your *rotis.*

Accept compliments like dowry: awkwardly and without question.

You can win awards, but if your *kheer* is too sweet or your tone too sharp, you're the villain in this *sanskari* serial.

In-Laws and the Art of Pretend Peace

Marriage is often marketed as a merger. But what they don't tell you is that the board of directors is a nosy WhatsApp group full of advice.

Every visit to the in-laws felt like a *reality show meets silent performance art.*

Mother-in-law (MIL): "You're looking well-fed. Must be happy."

Me: "Haha, yes! Happiness and *aloo paratha* are my personality now."

I could make sarcasm sound like Sanskrit. Polished. Poetic. Pretended.

Tupperware Diplomacy

I tried gifting peace through pickles. Homemade jam to win affection. Tupperware as tribute.

But there's no lid tight enough to contain insecurity. Or unsolicited advice.

MIL: "Have you thought of wearing more pastel? Strong colours make you look aggressive."

What I wanted to say:

"So does generational trauma. Should I tone that down too?"

What I did say:

"Of course, Aunty. Lavender it is."

"You know, we raised four kids without maids," her MIL said one day, sipping tea.

Ladoo sipped back. "And that's why therapy is trending now."

Her husband laughed.

Her MIL didn't.

Ladoo Singh's Journal: "Smile Mode Activated"

Burnt my hand while making *chai* for the fifth time today.

MIL said I make good tea when I don't talk too much.

Father-in-law (FIL) thinks I'm "modern" because I wear eyeliner and have opinions.

I smiled.

Because society loves *sanskari* robots in pretty packaging.

Scene: "How Can You Forget?"

MIL: "*Beta*, you forgot today is *Kanjak*!"

Ladoo: "Yes, Aunty, and also my own birthday. Priorities!"

FIL: "How can you forget such things? You women are meant to remember everything!"

Sure, Uncle. I remember:

Passwords.

Period dates.

Gas cylinder refill cycles.

Emotional trauma timelines.

But one *missed puja* and suddenly I'm *Bahu* #Fail.

Never mind that I hosted the last three, arranged the flowers, coordinated the prasad with the precision of a NASA launch, and still remembered to get *Kaka ji*'s gluten-free option. Never mind that I managed all this while juggling back-to-back calls, a project deadline, and a uterus that cramps like it's moonlighting as a medieval torture device.

But nope. I missed one.

And the echo chamber of joint-family righteousness exploded like I'd gate-crashed the *Kumbh Mela* in a miniskirt.

The irony?

Everything I do right is background noise. Expected. Normal. "What else would she do?"

But the moment I slip — forget a *puja*, burn a roti, say *"I'll join you later"* to a family WhatsApp video call, it's *breaking news. Sanskaari Bahu Turns Western: Film at 11.*

There's a part of me that sharpens her sarcasm like a *talwar.* I imagine saying:

"Oh, sorry, was I supposed to hang my achievements like mango pickles in the sun for validation?"

Or:

"Should I staple my promotion letter to the *ladoo* box next time so it counts as 'family contribution'?"

But then there's the other part.

The quieter one.

The one who's tired.

Tired of constantly being the diplomat, the scheduler, the soother, the sponge.

Tired of smiling when she wants to scream.

Tired of calculating the emotional interest she owes for every act of defiance, no matter how small.

So I stay silent.
Not because I agree.
But sometimes, the silence is less exhausting than the performance.

Her inner voice, weary but still standing, whispered:

"They remember the one time I didn't show up.
But they never counted the hundred times I did, without being asked."

The Meltdown Moment

One night, her baby had a fever. She cancelled a major presentation.
The client pulled out.
Her boss called it "unprofessional."
She rocked her child that night and whispered:
"Did I mess up?"
The baby gurgled and held her finger.
She realised:
She hadn't failed.

She had *chosen*.
And that was power.

Let's Talk About the Real Postpartum Symptoms

- ℵ Sleeplessness
- ℵ Crippling self-doubt
- ℵ Exploding diapers
- ℵ Random crying
- ℵ Overthinking every single decision
- ℵ Milk stains on every bra, top, and hope.

But no one talks about these.
Because women are supposed to "bounce back."
Like we're yoga balls.
They say a mother is born the day her child is.
No one says she also dies a little.
In my case, when the nurse handed me my daughter, I felt two things:

- ℵ Terror
- ℵ Constipation.

Welcome to post-partum glamour. Bollywood lied. No glowing cheeks. Just bleeding, stitches, and the kind of sleep-deprived delirium where you start calling your husband "Mama."

The Onset of Motherhood and Mayhem

The first week was a blur of nipples, nappies, and nausea. Every relative became a lactation expert. Even the ones who thought breastmilk was stored in the elbow.

Ma: "Eat *ghee laddoos, beta.* Milk *banega.*" (Eat these energy bites, darling – they are good for new mothers.")

Me: "Then why am I producing anxiety instead of Amul gold?"

The Boys' Club and Baby Pics

Office dude: "Why don't you talk about your baby more?"
Same dude: "She's always distracted. Probably can't handle pressure."

Damned if you do. Judged if you don't.

Another guy got praised for leaving early to pick up his daughter.
Me? I left at 6 and heard:
"Half day today?"

Motherhood isn't a weakness.
But the world treats it like an attendance issue.

The Existential Spreadsheet

Sometimes I opened Excel and asked myself:
"Are these pivot tables more important than bedtime cuddles?"

Then I reminded myself:
"I'm not choosing between roles. I'm choosing not to lose myself."

And honestly?
The only KPI I need is:

- Is my son fed?
- Am I still sane?

- ℵ Did I laugh at least once today?

The Baby Monitor That Monitored My Breakdown

Every time he cried, I ran.

What if he needs me? What if he thinks I'm a bad mom? What if he remembers I let him cry for 34 seconds?

I became his in-house Alexa. Except I didn't shut off.

Meanwhile, Silent Singh slept like a yogi in exile. Snored occasionally. Woke up to say, "You're doing great," then passed out again.

I hated him. I loved him. I also wanted to throw a diaper at his face.

The Judgment Parade

"You're breastfeeding, right?"

"Still co-sleeping?"

"You haven't started solids?"

"You're using formula?"

Every choice was a debate. Every deviation, a scandal. I began responding with:

"Thanks for your concern. Kindly take your judgment and shove it in a sterilised bottle."

Did I say that out loud? No. But the baby monitor heard it.

Silent Singh, My Sleep-Deprived Co-Founder

He once tried to burp the baby by playing Metallica. Did it work? No. Did I laugh for the first time in days? Yes.

That's the thing about him. He didn't fix the chaos. He sat with me in it.

One day I asked,

"Am I a bad mother?"

He said, "No. You're just finally a woman who stopped pleasing everyone."

Cue hormonal waterfall.

Society's Gold Medal for Martyrdom

Motherhood is the only job where, if you ask for a break, they say, "But it's a blessing."

Yes, Karen. Blessings don't cancel exhaustion. Try blessing your way through a colic episode at 2 am.

One day, I hid in the bathroom just to cry. Silent Singh knocked. "Everything okay?"

I replied, "Yes, just meeting my deadlines. Tears due by 5 pm."

He slid a chocolate under the door. That's love language when words don't work.

That day at work, everything that could go wrong did.

A tiny but critical mistake slipped through on the priority project — the kind that makes your stomach tie itself into knots and your inbox erupt with urgent messages.

I missed the morning meeting because the baby had decided 6 AM was the new midnight, and there was no winning that battle.

When I finally trudged back home, bleary-eyed and bruised by the day's chaos, the first thing waiting for me was a litany of complaints — the kind that could've been solved if someone just lifted a finger, but instead landed squarely on my shoulders.

That's when I cracked.

The pieces of me, once held together by stubbornness and caffeine, scattered like confetti in a storm.

And I decided: no more trying to be in ten places at once. No more being the superhero who never takes off the cape. No more apologies for needing a break.

The New Kind of Productivity

One day, Ladoo decided not to join that 9 PM call.

Instead, she made hot chocolate — the kind with just enough marshmallows to feel like a hug in a mug.

She read three pages of a book before the eyelids staged a peaceful rebellion and claimed victory.

And she kissed her baby goodnight, without once sneaking a peek at the glowing prison of unread emails.

She didn't feel lazy.

She felt human.

Like a little rebellion wrapped in cosy pyjamas, quietly reminding herself that sometimes, the bravest thing you can do is simply show up for yourself.

Writer's Perspective

We call working mothers superheroes. But we expect them to be superhuman.

To bounce back. Show up. Stay calm. And never complain.

This chapter is for every woman who wiped tears before opening her laptop.

For every mom who skipped pumping milk to meet a deadline.

You are not failing.

You are functioning.

And that's a miracle already.

Inner Voice Note

"You are not a bad mom for working. You are not a bad employee for mothering. You are just a woman refusing to disappear."

Chapter 7:

Fine. Just Kidding. I'm Not.

Or how Ladoo Singh smiled through breakdowns and learned to make peace with her pause button.

"Her silence wasn't emptiness. It was volume muted by society's expectations."

The Pause That Heals

They called her brave, yet never asked,
If the bravery came from a soul unmasked.
They called her strong, but strength runs dry.
When no one sees the tears she hides.
She paused one day, not to quit —
But to breathe in full and slowly, sit.
And in that breath, the silence spoke:
"You're not broken. You just awoke."

"ARE YOU OKAY?"

The question came often.

And Ladoo's answer was always the same — a polite smile, a nod, and two words she had mastered to say without blinking:

"I'm fine."

It was a lie she wore like lipstick — flawless, bright, and smudge-proof.

Because if she said she wasn't okay, someone might feel… uncomfortable.

So she adjusted her voice, her vibe, her volume, and carried on.

Until one day, her silence began to scream.

Corporate life is like a *tandoori paneer* wrap.

On the outside, it looks perfect. Inside, you're mostly burning.

I returned to work three months after maternity leave. My boss welcomed me like a returning war hero:

"Oh wow, you made it! So brave!"

Translation:

"We thought you'd disappear into the breastfeeding Bermuda Triangle."

The Return of the Working Mom

I came back with breast pads, under-eye circles, and a baby monitor app more active than my Outlook calendar.

In meetings, I nodded sagely while texting Silent Singh: "Did she poop today? How much? Describe consistency."

Colleagues said, "You're glowing!"
No, Priya. It's night sweats and leaked coffee.

The Boardroom Ballet

Being a working mom is a constant pirouette:

- ℵ Smile confidently.
- ℵ Apologise for nothing.
- ℵ Answer emails while breastmilk leaks through your satin shirt.

One time, I gave a client presentation with a diaper stuck to my laptop bag.

He didn't notice. Or pretended not to. Legend.

Another time, I was asked to "not bring motherhood to work." As if I could unzip my uterus and leave it in the lobby.

Appraisal Time: The Guilt Gets Promoted Too

Manager: "You've done well, but your travel commitment was a bit low this quarter."

Me: "Yes, I was busy keeping a human alive."

Apparently, Q4 doesn't include colic.

The Cult of Hyper-Moms

Some moms wake up at 4 AM to make beetroot *parathas* shaped like unicorns. Others wake up at 7:45, scream into the void, and serve cereal with questionable milk.

Guess which one I was?

School drop-offs felt like a fashion parade. There I was, wearing yesterday's eyeliner as war paint, waving at moms who looked like Pinterest boards.

The Dreaded Project Week

Nothing bonds parents like collective panic over art week.

Ladoo: "Let's do a volcano! Simple and classic."

Child: "I want a talking dragon that breathes actual fire."

Google, glue guns, glitter everywhere. Even Silent Singh got involved.

He asked, "Should we use baking soda or borrow from the chemistry lab?"

Me: "Let's not go to jail for fourth-grade homework."

Parent-Teacher Conference: The Real AGM

Teacher: "Your child is doing fine, but sometimes looks distracted."

I wanted to reply:

"Yes, she lives with me. Distraction is hereditary."

Instead, I smiled and nodded like a corporate trainee. Then spent the weekend spiralling: Am I a bad influence?

Silent Singh, The Homework Wingman

He's the guy who turned a cereal box into a solar system. The guy who said, "Marks don't define genius, but snacks do."

When I cried after seeing another mom's alphabet-shaped sandwiches, he said, "Our child eats food. That's enough alpha."

The Motherhood Comparison Olympics

- Her child is already reading *Harry Potter.*
- Mine is chewing on the book cover.
- She's enrolled hers in piano, robotics, and Mandarin.
- Mine knows all the lyrics to Baby Shark. In three languages.

Every win felt like my loss. Every brag typed in Arial felt like a punch in Comic Sans.

The Soundproof Suffering

Ladoo had mastered the art of invisible breakdowns.

She looked stunning in selfies, sounded confident in meetings, clapped at birthday parties, and replied with heart emojis in family WhatsApp groups.

But her real calendar?

- 3:00 AM: Anxiety
- 6:00 AM: Diaper duty
- 9:00 AM: Client call
- 12:30 PM: Overthinking
- 3:00 PM: PMS-fuelled impostor syndrome
- 6:00 PM: Passive guilt
- 9:00 PM: Scroll. Compare. Cry. Repeat.

Her therapist called it "emotional suffocation."
Her best friend called it "burnout."
Her mother called it "mood swings."
Ladoo called it **life on mute**.

The Day Ladoo Broke Down (in her car, silently)

It was a Wednesday.

A day that started with a promise. She had closed a deal, her smile genuine as she high-fived a client who actually seemed to mean it. She'd even remembered to send her husband's thyroid report, a small victory in the marathon of her responsibilities.

But the quiet pressure inside her, the weight she carried like an invisible backpack, was already gathering steam.

When her son came home that evening, holding up his drawing like a treasure, his voice full of hope and excitement, he said, "You weren't there when I showed my drawing."

She smiled — the kind of smile that's meant to soothe, to cover cracks, to promise that everything was okay.

"I'm proud of you, sweetheart," she said softly.

But the words felt hollow, even to her own ears.

Later, in the stillness of her car, stuck in the unforgiving crawl of evening traffic, the silence pressed in around her.

Her hands clenched the steering wheel, knuckles white. A quiet storm was brewing beneath her skin.

Frustration bubbled up, sharp and relentless, a pressure cooker of all the little things that had piled up: missed moments, unseen efforts, whispered doubts, and shouted expectations.

She wanted to scream at the world, at the day, at herself.

But all that escaped was a slow, silent leak of tears, falling unnoticed into the depths of her tote bag resting on the passenger seat.

In that suspended moment, the engine humming softly, the brake lights glowing red like quiet alarms, she felt the unbearable weight of trying to be everything for everyone.

Because the world applauds your balance, your ability to juggle work, home, and the chaos in between until your child's disappointment tips the scale and gravity pulls you under.

And there, in the stillness, the cracks showed.

Ladoo was not the unbreakable woman everyone expected her to be.

She was just human.

And in that stillness, with the city's noise fading into a distant hum, something inside her shifted.

Not with a bang, but with the softest whisper of rebellion.

Ladoo reached into her tote bag, fingers brushing against the worn spine of a book she'd been meaning to read for months. She pulled it out and traced the cover like a secret promise.

That night, she chose herself.

No 9 PM calls, no inbox avalanches, no endless apologies for needing a moment.

Instead, she made hot chocolate — thick, sweet, and generous with marshmallows, because if she was going to heal, it might as well be delicious.

She read three pages before her eyelids staged a peaceful takeover, and she surrendered to sleep like it was the greatest act of self-care.

And when she kissed her baby goodnight, she did it without glancing at her phone, without the background buzz of emails or expectations.

She didn't feel lazy.

She felt human.

And sometimes, that was enough

.

The Monster Called 'Mental Load'

It wasn't the baby.

It wasn't the boss.

It was the beast called *everything-at-once-ness.*

She was managing:

- Paediatrician appointments
- Grocery lists
- Office deadlines
- The maid's drama
- Her husband's sock shortage
- Her parents' sugar levels
- And everyone's emotional baggage.

She was the unpaid manager of life — no HR, no raise, no day off.

Her brain was a browser with 37 tabs open — one of them playing loud music, and she didn't know which.

The Letter to Her Inner Child

That night, she journaled. And for the first time, she wrote a letter to 10-year-old Ladoo.

Dear me,

I'm sorry I kept pushing you.

I turned you into a robot with lipstick.

I ignored your yawns and mocked your softness.

But you're not weak. You're wounded.

And I promise to rest with you. To breathe with you. To let you just be.

Signs She Wasn't 'Fine'

- She cried when a pasta ad played.
- She felt envious watching someone nap on Instagram.
- She fantasised not about beaches, but about turning off her phone.
- She laughed at jokes, but didn't feel joy.
- She missed herself. Not the pre-baby self. Not the pre-marriage self. Just… her.

The Quote That Changed Everything

Over tea one evening, her friend casually said:
"You don't have to do it all. There are no medals for burnout."
Ladoo froze.
No medals. Just migraines.
She wrote the quote on a sticky note and placed it on her fridge.
Every morning, it whispered:
"Survival is enough."

Silent Singh, COO of My Sanity

He packed lunches.
He did the laundry.
He Googled "how to soothe a teething baby" more than any paediatrician should.
One day, I broke down mid-Zoom call.
He handed me tea with a note:
"CEO of Everything. Please hydrate."
He didn't ask me to stop.
He held the fort, so I didn't have to burn it down.

She Started Saying No

No to PTA WhatsApp drama.
No to extra work with zero thanks.
No to meetups that drained her.
No to guilt dressed up as tradition.

She even told her in-laws, "I love you, but Sundays are now silent days. No planning. No expectations. Just pyjamas."

It caused a minor earthquake.

But her soul sighed with relief.

The Sacred 10 Minutes

She created a ritual.

Every day, she sat by the window. No phone. No guilt. Just her, a candle, and the chaos of her mind.

Sometimes she wrote. Sometimes she did nothing. Once, she just stared at a ceiling fan for ten minutes and felt **alive**.

The fan didn't judge.

The fan didn't care about postpartum belly folds or performance reviews.

She Didn't Need to Be Happy All the Time

She just needed space to be **honest**.

To say:

- "I'm tired."
- "I don't know."
- "I want to be alone."
- "I miss me."
- "I'm not okay."

Writer's Perspective

We live in a culture obsessed with "resilience."
But no one teaches us **release**.
Ladoo didn't break because she was weak.
She broke because she was **unheard**.
This chapter isn't about a meltdown. It's about *permission*, to feel, to rest, to scream softly and still be seen.
Sometimes, the bravest thing a woman can do is **pause**.

Inner Voice Note

"You can be grateful and still tired. You can love your life and still want a pause. Healing is not betrayal — it's survival."

Chapter 8:

Cape Off, Bra Off, Sanity On

Or how Ladoo Singh retired from being Superwoman and finally sat her glorious butt down.

"She dropped the cape, picked up courage, and suddenly, she could breathe again."

Cape No More

She flew for years without a map,
Dodging guilt in every gap.
She stitched her cape with duty's thread,
And wore it tight, though tears she shed.
But then one day, she hung it low,
And watched the wind begin to blow.
It didn't carry her away;
It whispered, "You're enough. Just stay."

NOBODY HANDS YOU a cape at birth. But if you're a woman, you're born into the expectation of one.

Be available. Be nice. Be perfect. Be invisible but look amazing doing it.

And once you become a mom or a wife or a manager or all three, the cape gets upgraded. Now it has deadlines, diaper bags, and *dalgona coffee anxiety*.

Ladoo Singh didn't sign up to be Superwoman.

But somehow, she became one.

The kind with bags under her eyes, guilt in her handbag, and a never-ending to-do list she mentally carried to bed.

And in that stillness, with the city's noise fading into a distant hum, something inside her shifted.

Not with fireworks, not with a grand announcement — just a quiet little spark of rebellion.

Because here's the truth: women like Ladoo don't really get a choice.

Want a career? Then you have to be flawless — a walking, talking LinkedIn success story who never misses a deadline or a networking brunch.

Want a happy family? Great! Now you're also the chef, the chauffeur, the therapist, and the designated Pinterest party planner.

Want to have a life *for yourself*? Ha! That's a side quest you sneak in between toddler tantrums and budget meetings, like a ninja in yoga pants.

Basically, being a woman means being Superwoman, except your cape is stained with coffee, your mask is smudged with baby food, and your superpower is somehow functioning on three hours of sleep and a prayer.

So, that night, when Ladoo reached into her bag and pulled out a book she'd been ignoring for months, it wasn't just about reading.

It was a tiny, fierce act of rebellion.

No 9 PM calls. No frantic inbox triage. No more apologising for just *being.*

She made hot chocolate, thick and sweet, loaded with enough marshmallows to feel like a warm hug from the universe.

She read three pages. Okay, maybe two and a half. Before sleep finally won the battle.

And when she kissed her baby goodnight, she did it without one glance at her buzzing phone.

She didn't feel lazy.

She felt human.

And in that simple truth, she found the strength to keep going, just as she was.

The Woman in the Mirror Cabin

They say we have it all now: equality, flexibility, empowerment.

But no one tells you how having it all comes with a footnote: *Does not include peace of mind, time to nap, or societal approval if you're not constantly grateful.*

I once attended a leadership summit while pumping milk in a five-star bathroom. That is not balance. That is plumbing.

Symptoms of Superwoman Syndrome

- Saying "I'm fine" with mascara halfway down your cheeks
- Feeling guilty for resting

- ℵ Forgetting when you last had a conversation that wasn't multitasked
- ℵ Apologising for not doing more, even when you're already running on crumbs.

She made organic snacks. Paid EMIs. Planned birthdays. Knew which medicine the maid's child needed. And remembered to smile during Zoom calls.

But if her kid had 11 minutes of screen time instead of 10?

Guilt.

Because perfection never gets a break.

Monologue: Ladoo vs. the Myth of 'Strong Woman'

You smile, you multitask, you even wear a saree without pinning it.

So, they assume you're sorted.

That your shoulders don't hurt from carrying expectations in invisible bags.

That if you're laughing at a joke, you're not choking inside.

Truth?

I laugh because it's safer than screaming.

Reflection: "The Problem with Being the Strong One"

They don't check on the strong ones.

They assume your lipstick is armour, not war paint.
They clap for your poise, not noticing your pulse.
But strength isn't the absence of struggle,
It's the audacity to still love, laugh, and live with honesty
when the world only applauds silence and subservience.

The Breaking Point

It was a Tuesday.

The kind of day where every sound seemed to gang up on her — the relentless whirr of the ceiling fan, the clatter of pots in the kitchen, the high-pitched shrill of her mother-in-law's "just asking" questions, and the unmistakable squish of mashed banana smeared liberally across her child's face.

Ladoo sat at the dining table, fingers trembling over the keyboard, trying to write an email that demanded her full attention. But the world around her was a messy symphony of chaos.

One hand fed the baby, slipping in clumps of banana with the precision of a juggler defying gravity.

The other stirred the *dal*, careful not to let it stick — a slow, soothing swirl in an otherwise frantic morning.

Her coffee sat dangerously close to the edge of the table, a second death looming if she didn't rescue it soon.

Meanwhile, her mother-in-law's voice floated over the noise like a persistent mosquito, "Are you eating enough? Is the baby sleeping well? Have you thought about *that* rishta proposal?"

Each question stacked on top of the last, a tower of tiny urgencies and expectations that Ladoo couldn't topple fast enough.

Her head buzzed; a thousand little voices, demands, and distractions crashing into one another, until the pressure inside her felt like it might burst.

And then, somewhere between the spoonful of *dal* and the fifth "just asking," she snapped.

A quiet, shattering snap that echoed in the stillness she desperately craved.

Because sometimes, even Superwoman has to let the cape fall.

"CAN I JUST BREATHE FOR A SECOND?!"

Her shoulders sagged under the weight of it all — the invisible burden of needing to be everywhere, for everyone, all at once.

And then, like a quietly thunderous crack, she snapped.

Not with a shout or a storm, but a breaking free of all the little pieces she'd been holding together.

Tears came then, unbidden and unapologetic, slipping freely now as she finally allowed herself to feel the ache beneath the exhaustion.

Her breath hitched.

A bittersweet smile flickered across her lips — fragile, weary, and utterly human.

This smile wasn't a victory. It was survival.

Her husband looked up from his laptop, eyebrows knitting in concern. "Are you okay, Ladoo?"

Her mother-in-law stiffened, her eyes darting between the child's banana-smeared face and Ladoo's trembling hands. "Maybe you need to eat something more… nutritious."

Her friend, who'd just dropped by, hesitated in the doorway, awkward smile faltering. "Want me to stay? Or maybe I can help with the baby?"

Ladoo swallowed hard, then let out a shaky laugh, the sound raw but real. "I'm fine. Just… multitasking gone rogue."

Her husband closed his laptop, moving to sit beside her. "You don't have to do it all."

The words hung in the air like a lifeline.

In that moment of quiet surrender, there was no shame.

Only the raw, unvarnished truth of being a woman — strong enough to keep going, fragile enough to break, and brave enough to start again.

Because sometimes, even Superwoman needs to put down her cape and just breathe.

Dear Diary, I Quit

That night, she sat with a notebook.
And wrote:
"I'm tired of being 'The Good Everything.'"
Good daughter. Good wife. Good mom. Good colleague.
She wanted to be *just* good. At being **herself**.

The Realisation

She wasn't chasing excellence.
She was running from *irrelevance*.
Afraid that if she stopped performing, she'd be forgotten.
Because our world doesn't applaud rest, it applauds results.
Even if you're rotting inside.

The Toxic Trio of Womanhood

- **Be Available.** To everyone. All the time. Even when your own tank's empty.
- **Be Beautiful**. But don't try too hard, that's vain.

ℵ **Be Better**. Than yesterday, than your peers, than that mom on Instagram with matching outfits and oat milk hacks.

Ladoo was done playing this impossible game.

Reflection: "When the Cape Feels Heavy"

Some nights, Ladoo wonders if she's doing enough.
Enough for her child. Her job. Her marriage. Herself.
And then she remembers:
She's not just working to earn. She's working to show her child what a woman can be.
Not perfect.
Not always present.
But powerful, real, and fiercely full of love.

Rebellion in Pyjamas

One Saturday, she made a radical decision.

She did nothing.

No dishes. No decked-up dinners. No digital detox yoga zooms. She stayed in her worn-out pyjamas — the ones with faded cartoons and a mysterious tea-stain shaped like Kerala, and made peace with the fact that they didn't spark joy, but they did spark freedom.

But rebellion isn't always loud. Sometimes it's a whisper that fights against decades of conditioning.

By 10:17 AM, she was itching.

Not physically, but emotionally. That anxious hum that came from years of being taught that stillness is laziness and rest is guilt. Her brain played games.

"Maybe just check one email…"

She reached for her phone.

Paused.

Put it under the cushion like it was a bar of chocolate during *Navratri.*

At 11:30, she saw the dust on the console table.

That one speck.

Mocking her like an in-law's passive-aggressive comment.

She stood up…

Then sat right back down.

"It can wait," she muttered.

It sounded foreign at first. Like speaking French in Math class.

But also, delicious.

By 1:00 PM, she started writing an imaginary apology to society. *Dear Everyone, I didn't cook a* thali *today. I reheated leftovers. I didn't 'freshen up' before lunch. I didn't wear a bra. Yes, I am still a good human.* She laughed to herself. Laughed so hard, she cried a little.

Because this was bigger than a nap.

This was a small, soft mutiny.

She wasn't being lazy.

She was recovering.

From being everything to everyone, all the time.

Inner voice, smug in stretchy waistbands, whispered:

"I wasn't born to chase dust bunnies and deadlines every day. Sometimes, even goddesses need pajamas and peace."

No cooking. No cleaning. No "let me quickly check."

She wore pyjamas. Put on a cracked face mask. Ate *chikki.* Watched cartoons.Her son joined. They laughed.

Her husband walked in, stunned. "What's happening?" She said, "A revolution."

He tiptoed around it and sat down.

That day wasn't Instagram-perfect. But it was real.

And real felt delicious.

The Cape Goes Off

That evening, she folded her imaginary cape.

Hung it next to her padded bra, expired guilt, and last year's resolutions.

She put on comfort instead.

She whispered:

"I'm not Superwoman. I'm a woman. And that is **more** than enough."

New Mantras

- ℵ Burnout isn't a badge.
- ℵ Saying NO is self-respect, not rebellion.
- ℵ Dusty shelves won't kill anyone. But internal clutter might.

- If they say you've changed, say thanks. That's called *evolving.*

She realised she didn't have to do it all.
Just do what made her feel **alive**.

Writer's Perspective

This chapter is not a rant. It's a revelation.

We romanticise Superwomen but forget they're usually sleep-deprived, self-neglecting, and silently sobbing behind bathroom doors.

Let's normalise:

- Asking for help
- Letting laundry pile up
- Cancelling plans because "I need to do nothing"
- And redefining strength not as *doing everything*, but as *knowing when to stop.*

Inner Voice Note

"The cape looks good, but it's choking you. Hang it up. Wear something comfortable instead, like peace, softness, or your own damn skin."

Chapter 9:

Guilt Trip – The Map Rewritten

Or how Ladoo finally swapped her baggage for a backpack

Guilt Stamps on My Passport

Nine stops, nine sighs, nine teary laughs,
Through mirrors, medals, and messy drafts.
Each guilt a visa I thought I owed,
Till I found joy off the beaten road.
Now I carry truth, not weight,
And guilt? Just a boarding gate.

IF GUILT WERE a loyalty program, I'd have earned lifetime platinum.

I could start a travel agency called *WanderLadoo: Tours of Emotional Turmoil.* Because I took all the guilt trips. Twice.

Body guilt. Rishta rejection guilt. Trophy-seeking guilt. Being-a-woman guilt. Career guilt. Motherhood guilt. Miscarriage guilt. WhatsApp-group guilt.

But here's what I learned: Guilt isn't always your enemy. It's a GPS. It tells you what matters. It just doesn't know when to shut up.

Nine Postcards From the Pitstops

ℵ

ℵ **Guilt in a Mirror Frame**
Don't shrink your shine to fit the size chart.
Beauty isn't a reward for weight loss.

ℵ I still remember that mirror in my teenage room. It didn't reflect me. It judged me. If that mirror could talk, it would've said, "Stand sideways. Suck in your stomach. And while you're at it, suck in your joy too."

ℵ **Guilt in a Trophy Cabinet**
Excellence is great. Exhaustion is not a metric.
If you lose sleep for applause, it's not success. It's a sacrifice.

ℵ When the lights go off and the audience claps fade, what remains is the echo of your own unmet need for rest. I once dreamt of failing a test just to see if I would survive the silence. Spoiler: I would've. But I never dared.

- ℵ **Guilt in a Biodata Folder**
  Being "marriage material" shouldn't mean being flammable. You're not a *rishta* product. You're a person with taste.
- ℵ There were days I felt like I was being auctioned in slow motion. Educational background? Check. Culinary skills? Check. Waistline? Negotiable. Dowry? Let's just call it "cultural expectations."
- ℵ **Guilt in a Smile Mask**
  Being polite isn't peace. Performing strength is not strength. You can say "I'm not okay" and still be enough.
- ℵ The myth of the smiling woman is older than the Himalayas. Especially when she's an in-law. You can either be liked or be yourself. But not both. Until you realise that being disliked by the right people is freedom.
- ℵ **Guilt in a Baby Monitor**
  Motherhood is not martyrdom. Your kid needs you to be happy, not perfect.
- ℵ I once cried because I forgot to pack her favourite spoon. I also once forgot her lunch altogether. And she still survived. Guilt will tell you you're failing every minute. Love will remind you that you're still here, trying.
- ℵ **Guilt in an Empty Womb**
  You are allowed to grieve what never was.
  Loss without form is still loss with meaning.
- ℵ We don't light candles for unborn dreams. We stuff them into sentences like "It wasn't meant to be." But grief doesn't expire, and neither does the love you imagined giving.
- ℵ **Guilt in a Job Appraisal**
  The glass ceiling isn't shatterproof, but your spirit is. You're not split in two; you're stretched in brilliance.
- ℵ Corporate guilt is wearing lipstick over fatigue and selling ideas you birthed in between midnight feeds. It's being told you're too emotional in one breath and too cold in another. Its performance wrapped in pant-suit diplomacy.

- ℵ **Guilt in a WhatsApp Group**
  Muting the world isn't quitting. It's curating.
  Choose your peace over perfection.
- ℵ Motherhood is now a scoreboard. Every message feels like another round of gladiator parenting. I once saw a mom post a 5-layer gluten-free bento box and cried over my child's banana with a bite mark from last night.
- ℵ **Guilt in a Luggage Scanner**
  Guilt isn't proof you care. Healing is.
- ℵ At the airport of life, you carry more than handbags. You carry fears, regrets, should-haves, and not-enoughs. But now, I travel lighter. I pack joy. I check in with grace.

Silent Singh, My Unpaid Therapist

He never fixed me. He sat with me.

He made space. Not solutions.

When I broke down at 2 AM because our son had a fever, he said, "Let me take the second shift." When I cried about missing an off-site promotion dinner, he sent me a screenshot of her smiling with a caption: "This. Is. Better."

Sometimes he said nothing. Just passed the ketchup. Healing isn't always a TED talk. Sometimes, it's tea.

Takeaways for Fellow Travellers

- ℵ You are not late. You are layered.
- ℵ You are not broken. You're blooming.
- ℵ You can be both proud and healing.
- ℵ You can parent and pause.
- ℵ You can change your script mid-scene.
- ℵ You can stop explaining.
- ℵ You don't owe anyone an edited version of your becoming.
- ℵ You can forgive yourself without asking for permission.
- ℵ You can mute guilt the way you mute WhatsApp groups: with intention.
- ℵ You are not a role. You are a revolution.

Writer's Note

If you saw yourself in these chapters, welcome. You are the co-author.

You don't need a passport to start a guilt trip. But to come back? That takes strength.

Here's the thing: guilt only survives in the dark. Shine light on it with laughter, tears, poetry, silence, therapy, samosas, or whatever it takes.

You don't need to be perfect. You just need to be present.

And if you're reading this, you're already home.

Chapter 10:

Permission Denied, Peace Achieved

Or how Ladoo Singh made "No" her new love language.

"She built fences not to keep people out, but to keep her peace in."

Permission Denied, Peace Achieved

She used to nod, to please, to smile,
To walk the extra, unseen mile.
Her voice was soft, her tone was low,
She only whispered every no.
But then she stood, no guilt, no fear,
And made her silence crystal clear.
She said: "I choose my peace, my voice."
And walked away — her loudest choice.

THERE COMES A day in every woman's life when she realises that her biggest enemy is not failure, not cellulite, not that one ex who still stalks her silently on Instagram.

It's **approval addiction.**

Ladoo Singh was the gold-medal winner of the Approval Olympics.

From age five, she was conditioned to be the "good girl" — agreeable, grateful, flexible, and deeply apologetic for simply existing in a body with opinions.

She said yes when she meant maybe. She said maybe when she meant absolutely not.

She smiled when she was simmering. Until one day, she didn't.

Yes Was Her Default Mode

- "Can you cover for me?" Yes.
- "Can you make it to the *puja*?" Yes.
- "Can you help with this presentation by EOD?" Yes.
- "Can you ignore the fact that we treat you like a backup plan and a human task list?" Of course, yes!

Because saying no was never an option.

Saying no meant drama. It meant conflict. It meant *disapproval.*

Ladoo was allergic to disapproval. Her whole life was built on applause.

Even if it was the kind that came with a heavy sigh.

The Day She Said It

It was an innocent request.

A neighbourhood aunty wanted her to come speak at a kitty party about "how to balance it all."

She laughed. Out loud.

Balance?

She hadn't clipped her toenails in two weeks. Her child was eating cereal with a spatula. Her husband had worn mismatched socks for three days and blamed the maid.

And still, she almost said yes.

Until something in her paused.

And she typed back one word:

"No."

Followed by: "But thank you. I'm currently balancing my mental health. It's wobbly enough."

What Followed Was Not Peace

It was chaos.

People were shocked. Appalled.

Even offended.

"You've changed," someone said.

"You were always so helpful."

"Why so rude?"

But Ladoo had learned something new:

Saying no doesn't make you rude. It makes you real.

Types of "No" Ladoo Mastered

- ℵ **The Polite Professional No**
  "Thank you for considering me, but I won't be able to commit to this right now."
- ℵ **The Personal Space No**
  "I love you, but I need time alone. Let's talk tomorrow?"
- ℵ **The Social Media No**
  (Turned off notifications. Didn't respond. No guilt. Revolutionary.)
- ℵ **The Family Drama No**
  "I will not attend another event where my weight is discussed like a weather report."

How Her World Reacted

- ℵ Some were confused.
- ℵ Some were irritated.
- ℵ Some were suddenly distant.

And that's when Ladoo realised that boundaries are like bouncers.

They don't keep *you* out.

They keep the wrong energy from barging in with shoes on.

But it wasn't easy.

Because the moment she started saying **no**, another voice — older, deeper, softer —rose inside her.

The voice of every woman before her who had kept the peace at the cost of her own.

It said, *"Just one yes won't hurt."*

"Don't be difficult."
"What if they think you're selfish?"

She stared at the message on her phone — another *"Can you quickly jump on a call?"* on a Sunday.
Her finger hovered over the screen.
She could hear her own breath. Her heartbeat. Her doubt.

Then, slowly, she put the phone down.
No means no, she whispered.
Even if it's whispered.
Even if it's followed by a thousand nervous heartbeats.
Even if it makes people uncomfortable.
She wasn't being rude. She was being real.
Because the people who love you conditionally?
They only stay as long as you keep shrinking.
The ones who love you truly?
They stretch with you.
They stay even when your "no" echoes louder than your smile.

Inner Voice Note:

"You don't owe anyone access to the parts of you they refuse to respect."

Aunties vs Boundaries

One aunty once commented at a wedding, "*Beta*, you didn't bring anything homemade?"

Ladoo replied:

"No, Aunty. I brought myself. Freshly bathed. That's all I could manage."

She smiled. Walked off.

Didn't look back.

It felt better than a spa day.

No Is a Full Sentence

It doesn't need:

- ℵ "I'm sorry but…"
- ℵ "Actually, I would have, but…"
- ℵ "Hope you understand…"

Sometimes, you say it.

And breathe.

Because every yes you give away from guilt is a no to your peace.

The Freedom of Filters

Ladoo applied the same rule online.

She unfollowed people who made her feel less.

She muted relatives who DM'd diet plans.

She posted messy, happy, real moments, and didn't check likes.

The Breakthrough Moment

One day, her son asked:
"Mama, why do you always say yes when you're tired?"
She paused. Looked into his eyes.
And said, "Because I forgot I was allowed to say no."
Then she hugged him and whispered:
"You're allowed too. Always."

Writer's Perspective

The word "No" has been villainised in women.
We're told it's selfish, cold, rude, too bold, not nurturing.
But here's the truth:
"No" is **self-love in syllables**.
This chapter isn't about rebellion.
It's about *reclaiming your right to rest, refuse, and be real.*

Inner Voice Note

"Every time you say yes to please someone, ask yourself: are you abandoning yourself to do it?"

Chapter 11:

Dreams, Desires & Dosas

Or how Ladoo Singh dared to want more, and didn't apologise for it.

"She stopped asking for permission and started asking for extra chutney instead."

Poem: Dreams, Desires & Dosas

She dreamed in lists and laundry loads,
Of places far from known zip codes.
Of books unwritten, songs unsung,
A version of her is still young.
They said, "Too late." She said, "Not yet."
She chased her fire with no regret.
A dosa crisp, a soul so wide,
She finally tasted her own side.

THEY SAY DESIRE is dangerous.

Especially when it belongs to a woman.

Especially if she's already married, already a mother, already successful, already "settled."

But Ladoo Singh had a secret:

She wanted more.

Not just extra *sambhar* with her *dosa.*

Not just uninterrupted sleep (though yes, please).

She wanted *more of herself* back.

Her dreams hadn't expired. They were just shelved next to baby formula and family WhatsApp forwards.

And she was ready to dust them off.

The Day She Admitted It

It started with a *dosa.*

She was at a café, eating alone — a rare miracle.

The waiter asked, "Plain or *masala*?"

And she said, "Masala."

Ladoo stared down at the dosa menu like it held the secrets to a better day.

Her mind wandered to the possibilities. The golden crispiness, the tangy chutney, the gooey stretch of melted cheese that usually felt like a forbidden luxury.

There was a voice in her head, quick and sharp like a well-trained drill sergeant, whispering, *"Too fattening. Too childish. Too expensive."*

But today, she shrugged off the chorus of cautions and restrictions.

Life was too short, too messy, too unpredictable to live in a constant waiting room, counting calories and compromises like they were tickets to happiness that might never come.

After all, she thought, *it's just a* dosa.

If it brought her joy, even a small spark of it, why not go for those extra things? The cheese, the *chutney*, the extra crisp edge that crackled like a tiny celebration.

She paused, savouring the thought, then smiled to herself and said aloud, "With cheese. And *chutney*. And extra crisp."

It was a small thing, but in that moment, it felt enormous.

Because for the first time in weeks, she was ordering exactly what she wanted, not what was convenient, acceptable, or less messy.

The Desire to Write Again

Before spreadsheets and spit-up cloths, Ladoo had been a writer.

She wrote poetry. Short stories. Sarcastic rants that could spark revolutions.

But somewhere between meetings and milestones, the pen dried up.

One day, her son asked, "Mama, what do you love doing?"

She didn't have an answer.

So she found a notebook.

And wrote one sentence:

"I want to want again."

The Checklist That Never Ended

Ladoo was always chasing completion:

- ℵ Job? Check.
- ℵ Marriage? Check.
- ℵ Baby? Check.
- ℵ Monthly goals? Check.
- ℵ Inner joy? … buffering.

She had learned to be grateful — constantly, loudly, endlessly. But somewhere in all that gratitude, she'd muted desire.

Because wanting more made you sound greedy.
Or ungrateful.

Or worse, *too much.*

But maybe "too much" was exactly what she was meant to be.

She had learned to be grateful — constantly, loudly, performatively.
Like, gratitude was a job description.

Thank you for this meal. Thank you for this opportunity. Thank you for tolerating me. Thank you for letting me breathe your air.

She could write a thesis titled *"How to Be Grateful and Shrink Yourself in Five Easy Steps."*

Step one: Smile.

Step two: Accept the bare minimum like it's divine grace.

Step three: Never, *ever*, say you want more.

Because somewhere in all that gratitude, she'd muted **desire**.

Because wanting more?

That was greedy.

That was unbecoming.

That was *ambition dressed in heels and a loud mouth*, and god forbid a woman be both hungry *and* well-heeled.

She'd seen it too often — the way women who dared to ask were labelled:

Too loud.
Too needy.
Too bold.
Too full of themselves.

But here's the cosmic joke: Ladoo had always been too much.

Too emotional. Too opinionated. Too damn alive.

And after years of sucking in her stomach *and* her personality at dinner tables and boardrooms, she was done.

Maybe "too much" wasn't a flaw.

Maybe it was her superpower.

Because it takes a hell of a lot of strength to want unapologetically.

To say, *"I deserve this"* without a footnote.

To ask for more space, more respect, more *sambhar*, without looking over your shoulder.

Inner Voice Note:

"You weren't born to be polite wallpaper.
You were born to take up space, spill some *chai*, and still be invited back."

The Wild Idea

She wanted to travel.
Alone.
Not for a conference.

Not for a wedding.

Not even for a spiritual reset.

Just… for silence, novelty, and a hot cup of tea she didn't have to reheat three times.

Ladoo didn't decide to travel alone on a whim.

It came quietly, not like a lightning bolt, but like a slow seep of water under a locked door. A knowing that crept in, one unnoticed moment at a time.

One evening, she was folding laundry — tiny socks, her husband's shirts, her mother-in-law's shawl — and realised her hands had memorised everyone else's needs. But not her own.

She cooked meals tailored to everyone's taste. Managed calendars that didn't include her name. Smiled through fatigue. Scheduled joy for others like it was her job, and forgot what hers looked like.

She gave so much comfort, so much care, and poured herself out like a bottomless jug — warm, steady, never spilling.

But one night, staring blankly at her reflection while brushing her teeth, a question whispered through the steam on the mirror:

When was the last time you did something just for *you*?

She couldn't remember.

Not a chore, not a compromise, not a "maybe next weekend" plan with someone else's comfort in mind, but something just for the sheer, selfish, delicious thrill of it.

And so the idea began. Not as an escape, but as a reclamation.

A trip. Not to prove a point or run away, but as a gift to herself. A soft rebellion. A thank you note to her soul.

To wake up without an alarm clock. To sip coffee slowly, watching strangers instead of emails. To eat meals that didn't ask, "What will they think?" To wander new streets without dragging guilt like a carry-on.

For once, she wouldn't be someone's mother, daughter, wife, manager, problem-solver, or peacekeeper.

She'd just be Ladoo.

And that, she thought, would be more than enough

She floated the idea gently at dinner.

Her husband choked on his *roti*.

"But… why? Without us?"

She smiled.

"Exactly."

The Guilt Came, Of Course

Guilt is clingy like a too-tight bra on a humid day.

- "How can you leave your child?"
- "What if something happens?"
- "What kind of mother needs a break?"

To which Ladoo answered (in her head first, and then out loud):

"The kind who is one tantrum away from becoming a meme."

She booked a two-day retreat in the hills.

Told no one until it was time to pack.

It wasn't brave. It was **necessary**.

That One Dinner Party

At a get-together, someone said:
"Oh, you're going on a solo trip? That's nice. I wish I could, but you know, responsibilities."

Ladoo sipped her wine.
"Same. I'm just taking my responsibilities with me. In the form of a journal and some vitamin D."

Mic. Dropped. Sip.

She Wanted It All

Not the "Lean In" corporate ladder poster kind of all.
Her all was personal:

- ℵ To work part-time
- ℵ To bake messy cakes
- ℵ To nap without shame
- ℵ To wear lipstick for no one
- ℵ To dream big and fail happily.

She wanted to live a life that felt like *hers*, not a brochure for balanced living.

Writer's Perspective

Desire isn't the enemy.
Deadlines are.

Ladoo Singh reminded herself that wanting more didn't mean she was lacking in love. It meant she was listening to her soul.

This chapter is for the women who forgot they could want without guilt.

It's for the women whose dreams aren't dead, just drowsy.

Inner Voice Note

"You don't have to earn rest. Or joy. Or a second *dosa.* You just have to want it."

Chapter 12:

Unapologetically Under Construction

Or how Ladoo Singh learned that becoming isn't a race. It's a lifelong renovation project.

"She wasn't flawless. But she was fearless in her becoming."

Unapologetically Under Construction

She painted walls, then brushed them bare,
Broke bricks she'd laid with tender care.
No blueprint drawn, no map, no chart.
Just doubt and breath, a beating heart.
She stitched her soul in quiet thread,
With dreams half-grown, and words unsaid.
Not fixed, but fierce. She came to be
A wild, bold work: becoming **she**.

THE REAL TIPPING point wasn't loud. It wasn't a fight or a dramatic meltdown. It was over toothpaste.

Her son had squeezed the tube from the middle again. Her husband had left the bathroom light on. Her mother-in-law shouted from the kitchen, "Ladoo, the *atta*'s finished!"

And Ladoo stood there, toothbrush in hand, staring at the mirror like it was a stranger.

She hadn't brushed her hair. She'd reheated her tea four times. She had half an email drafted, a damp towel on the bed, and three people waiting on her for completely different things.

Something clenched in her chest. Not pain, but the pressure of invisibility.

She didn't shout. She didn't cry. She just... stopped.

She walked out, towel still wrapped around her head, sat on the sofa, opened her laptop, and searched:

"Places to travel solo in India – quiet, no group tours, decent Wi-Fi."

Because in that moment, she realised something unsettling but true:

Everything she did, every minute of every day, was for someone else's comfort.

Their lunch preferences. Their calendars. Their mood swings. Even her smallest joys —what to eat, when to sleep, what show to watch —were filtered through someone else's convenience.

She hadn't done anything *just* for herself in years.

And so, she decided this one thing would be hers.

Not dramatic. Not angry. Not even particularly expensive. Just a few days.

Just her.

A quiet goodbye to her endless role-play, and a soft hello to the woman she used to know.

We're taught to aim for the final version of ourselves.

The perfect woman.

The glowing, healed, balanced, spiritual, smooth-skinned, Pinterest-level woman who drinks lemon water and wakes up with motivation instead of a neck cramp.

But Ladoo Singh?

She was a glorious mess in progress.

And she finally stopped apologising for it.

The Pressure to Be "Done"

At 32, Ladoo felt the weight of a thousand shoulds.

- ℵ You should have it all figured out.
- ℵ You should be happier.
- ℵ You should meditate.
- ℵ You should stop complaining.
- ℵ You should try keto.
- ℵ You should "just think positive."

She wanted to print a T-shirt that said:
"Still figuring it out. Don't @ me."

Because if life were a syllabus, no one had sent her the last chapter.

The Constant Self-Improvement Loop

There was always a new book, podcast, workshop, morning routine, journaling prompt, or gut cleanse claiming to "fix" her.

But what if she wasn't broken?

What if she were just **becoming**?

Like a house with scaffolding — not ugly, just mid-construction. Still home. Still whole.

Still worthy of warmth and Wi-Fi.

Healing Isn't Linear (Neither is Her Life)

Some days, she felt grounded.

Other days, she felt like a misplaced PDF file — open in 3 tabs, half-read, and freezing everything else.

But she stopped expecting perfection.

Instead, she made space for:

- Tiny wins
- Unfinished to-do lists
- Mood swings
- Days when brushing her hair was the main achievement.

She called them "emotionally productive" days.

Instagram Said: Glow Up. Ladoo Said: Nap First.

Every influencer screamed routines, rituals, and radiance.

Ladoo? She chose recovery.

She unfollowed perfection and followed women who talked about real stuff, like rage-cleaning, hormonal bloating, and why self-care sometimes looks like eating Maggi in silence at 11:43 PM.

She Outgrew People Too

Growth isn't just a solo journey. It's a luggage check.
And some people were baggage.
The friend who only called when she had gossip.
The cousin who made weight jokes wrapped in "concern."
The ex who still liked her selfies at 2 AM but never her progress.
She didn't hate them. She just… logged out.

The "I'm Still Learning" List

She was still learning to:

- Receive compliments without deflecting
- Ask for help without shame
- Sit with discomfort without scrolling
- Speak up in meetings without overexplaining
- Look in the mirror without zooming in on flaws
- Forgive herself. Repeatedly.

And the biggest?

To grow slowly. Loudly. Softly. In whatever way felt honest.

Unapologetically Under Construction

Once, someone said, "You've changed."
She smiled.
"Thank God."

She didn't want to be the woman who tolerated everything for peace.
She wanted to be the woman who created peace by walking away.

She didn't want to be the woman who made everyone comfortable.
She wanted to be the woman who made herself comfortable in her own skin.

She wasn't complete.

She was **becoming**.

And there was no deadline.

Writer's Perspective

This chapter is for the woman in the middle of her "what next?"

The woman who feels like a glitch in a world that demands polished updates.

You are not late.

You are not behind.

You are not a failure.

You are a beautiful, breathing version update in progress. Let the download take time.

Inner Voice Note

"You don't have to bloom in spring. Some souls flower in autumn. And that's still blooming."

Epilogue:

Lost & Found – The Self She Left Behind

Or how Ladoo Singh unpacked her guilt, folded it with grace, and finally found her way home.

"She didn't seek validation anymore. She became her own proof."

Her Luggage, Unpacked

She carried guilt like morning dew,
Unseen, but soaked in every hue.
It crept in dreams, it crept in day,
Till she decided —not today.
She dropped the bag, untied the knot,
Embraced the self the world forgot.
No more disguise, no filtered frame.
She wore her soul, and signed her name.

THERE WAS NO dramatic monologue.

No spotlight.

No Beyoncé background track.

Just a regular morning.

Sunlight through the curtain.

The kettle was humming.

And Ladoo Singh was standing in front of her mirror. Not to check for flaws, but to greet her reflection like a long-lost friend.

She wasn't flawless.

She wasn't fixed.

But for the first time in years, she wasn't at war with herself.

She was… home.

The Suitcase She'd Dragged For Years

We all carry invisible luggage.

Ladoo's came with a 'fragile' sticker and way too many baggage tags.

But that morning, she decided to finally unzip it.

Not to repack.

Not to organise.

Just to unpack.

One guilt at a time.

And to whisper to each:

"You've overstayed your visa. It's time."

The Nine Guilt Bags and the Poems They Carried

1. The Guilt of Being the 'Moti' Girl

She wasn't born with shame.
It was stitched into comments, wrapped in concern, and served at family dinners.

Poem:

They pinched her pride and poked her frame,
Called her sizes, not her name.
But beauty bloomed where shame was thrown,
And now her skin feels like her own.

2. The Guilt of Being Loud and Opinionated

They told her to "tone it down," as if her voice came with a volume warning.
But silence never saved her.

Poem:

Her voice once shrank to fit the room,
Until it cracked and broke the gloom.
Now, when she speaks, the world aligns;
She fills her space, redraws the lines.

3. The Guilt of Academic Perfectionism

She topped the charts but flunked the rest.
Trophies sat heavy on shelves and heavier on her shoulders.

Poem:

A+ grades and sleepless nights,
Medals polished, inner fights.
But now she knows: her worth's not scored.
It's how she breathes, not what she's stored.

4. The Guilt of Rejecting Rishtas

She said no to men who wanted a mould, not a woman. Every "no" was a yes to herself.

Poem:

She served the tea, not her soul,
Refused to dim to make love whole.
No wedding band, no pity sighs;
Just self-respect that never lies.

5. The Guilt of Choosing Work Over Rituals

She missed weddings for work, skipped fasts for deadlines, and heard the whispers.

Poem:

She skipped a prayer, skipped the scorn,
Said no to guilt she'd never worn.
And found her peace not in the shrine,
But in the "yes", she drew from her spine.

6. The Guilt of Not Enjoying Motherhood Every Minute

There were days she adored her child.
And days she wanted to run.
Both were true. And valid.

Poem:

A lullaby sung through gritted teeth,
A hug that healed, a sigh beneath.
Motherhood's not all joy and glee —
It's raw, it's real, it's mess-free.

7. The Guilt of Wanting Space

Sometimes, she locked herself in the bathroom. Not to cry.

Just to breathe.

Poem:

A door shut tight, the world on hold,
A moment warm when life felt cold.
She wasn't rude, she wasn't mean.
Just carving out her sacred scene.

8. The Guilt of Being Too Much and Never Enough

Too emotional. Too bold. Too quiet. Too loud.
She was tired of being edited.

Poem:

They trimmed her edges, shaped her tone,
Until her self felt not her own.
But now she blooms in untamed hues,
And picks herself. No need to choose.

9. The Guilt of Healing

She stopped chasing closure.
She chose compassion.
Not everyone got a goodbye.
Some just got silence.

Poem:

To heal is not to tie each knot,
Or fix each crack the world forgot.
It's learning rest, it's letting go,
And saying no without a show.

What Remains

Ladoo didn't become guilt-free.
She became **guilt-aware**.

She knew the difference now:

- ℵ Between inherited shame and earned wisdom.
- ℵ Between expectation and expression.
- ℵ Between shrinking and evolving.

Some guilt, she let go of.
Some she folded neatly.

Some she burned.
And some, she turned into boundaries.

Silent Singh's Final Word (And He Only Speaks In 4 Words)

At the end of all this, Silent Singh finally said, "You did it, Ladoo."

That's it. That's the whole review. Better than Goodreads.

He did say one more thing, though, which I now use as a mantra: "Guilt doesn't raise children. Love does."

And that applies to everything.

Truth Bombs Dressed as Jokes

Here's the thing. The world tells women:

- Be soft, but not a doormat.
- Be strong, but not rude.
- Be ambitious, but don't scare the boys.
- Be moms, but don't miss meetings.
- Be thin, but not too vain.
- Be confident, but humble.

This is not advice. This is *emotional CrossFit.*

If I followed every instruction given to me, I'd be a sugar-free gulab *jamun*: presentable but sad inside.

So I stopped. I broke up with guilt. We were toxic. And like every dramatic breakup, I posted about it. Hence, this book.

Writer's Perspective

The end of this book isn't about Ladoo becoming perfect.

It's her becoming real.

This epilogue isn't a ribbon-tied conclusion.

It's a quiet rebellion, that you don't have to wait for applause to claim your space.

Ladoo's journey ends here, but yours?

It may just be beginning.

If you've made it this far, first of all, congratulations. You've survived me. That alone qualifies you for sainthood or at least a guilt-free *jalebi.*

Secondly, this is where I remove the filter, spill the *chai*, and tell you what all this drama was really about.

Because let's admit it. Guilt is not a feeling. It's a *freaking industry.* From aunties who market shame like MLM schemes to the voice in your head that sounds suspiciously like your childhood piano teacher.

I didn't write this book to be wise. I wrote it because I was *tired of performing perfection and calling it growth.*

Final Inner Voice Note

"You are not what the world made you feel guilty for.
You are what you rise from.
What you reclaim.
And what you refuse to apologise for anymore."

You, Dear Reader, Are the Ladoo

Yes. You. This wasn't a memoir. This was a mirror.
If you've ever:

- ℵ Felt you were too much or not enough
- ℵ Skipped your story to play a side role in someone else's
- ℵ Looked in the mirror and wished for a filter
- ℵ Smiled through a storm and said, "I'm fine".
- ℵ Then congratulations. You are the main character.
- ℵ And guilt? That's just the background score we forgot to mute.

Word Cracker Ending: For the Logophiles and the Lost

Consider this your emotional palimpsest, a lexicon of liberation, a veritable smorgasbord of societal satire seasoned with schadenfreude and sprinkled with subaltern sass.

Still with me? Splendid. Because the truth is: *Ladoo is not just a person — Ladoo is a paradigm.*

She is the zany, zealous, zeitgeist of your forgotten dreams. She is the man who suppresses tears at appraisal meetings. She is the woman quietly gulping her ambition with *sabzi*.

She is you. Yes, you, with your emotional rollercoaster and WhatsApp anxiety and cupboard full of half-done diaries.

So let me be the first to say:

Congratulations. You have just arrived.

GLOSSARY: If You're Not Desi, Don't Worry – We Got You!

(A handy cheat-sheet for those wondering if 'Ladoo' is a person or a sweet. It's both.)

Jalebi – twisted sugar swirls

Beta – term of endearment for a younger person

Ragi – grain flour

Motu – fat, chubby

Golu – round

Gajar ka halwa – carrot-milk fudge

Maasi – aunt

Lehengas – embellished/bridal skirts

Rishta – matrimony offer/proposal

Gulab jamun – syrupy dumplings

Aloo tikki – spiced potato medallions

Pani puri – tangy street snacks

Dupatta – scarf/stole

Papad – crunchy lentil thins

Chachu – uncle

Puja – prayer

Shaadi – wedding

Thodi – just a pinch/slightly

Rasmalai – cream-soaked cottage cheese discs

Chutney – zesty herb spread

Ladki Dejhne ka season – the matchmaking months

Mundan – baby's ceremonial haircut

Sanskari – traditionally groomed

Khakhra – thin, crispy snack

Haldi doodh – turmeric infused milk

Kheer – rice pudding

Aloo paratha – stuffed potato flatbread

Kanjak – Goddess girl ritual

Kaka ji – uncle

Kumbh Mela – grand spiritual gathering

Ladoo – a sweet

Tandoori Paneer – marinated cheese cubes

Atta – wholemeal dough

Sabzi – home style vegetable curry

Acknowledgements

To every experience that etched its lesson on my heart, each joy, each sorrow, each imperfect, necessary moment, thank you for shaping me into someone braver and truer.

To all those whose paths have crossed mine, be it friends, teachers, or kind strangers, thank you for your light.

To my parents, my first heroes and forever confidants, your love is the compass that guides me home.

To my brother, thank you for standing beside me, steadfast and true, in ways words cannot fully hold.

To Shlok, Shaurya, and Shanaya, your laughter fills the hollow spaces with joy, and your love reminds me daily of all that is good and pure.

This book carries pieces of each of you, woven with gratitude, anchored in love, and lifted by faith.

About the Author

Dr. Rajani Tewari is a professional juggler of many hats: author, HR leader, accidental philosopher, and full-time mom to three delightful whirlwinds named Shlok, Shaurya, and Shanaya.

Armed with a sharp wit, a tender heart, and an abiding faith in Lord Shiva, she has spent her life collecting stories, learning from spectacular missteps, and occasionally triumphing over her own self-doubt.

Her writing is equal parts confessional and celebratory; a reminder that life rarely follows a script, and thank goodness for that. She believes in laughter as medicine, authenticity as a superpower, and the quiet conviction that no one is ever truly alone in their struggles.

When she isn't penning her thoughts or transforming workplaces with compassion and strategy, you'll likely find her sipping chai, plotting her next adventure, or trying to convince her children that "five more minutes" of quiet is a perfectly reasonable request.

This book is her love letter to every imperfect soul who is still learning to dance with their own story.